THERE ARE SOME THINGS THAT CHIP HARRISON WON'T DO

True, he is willing to move in circles that operate on what can only be called the wrong side of the law.

True, he is willing to do a star turn as a porno performer when the price is right.

True, he is willing to betray the man who is the best friend he has in the world when that man's wonderfully wanton wife makes him a proposition he cannot refuse.

True, he is willing to do practically anything to survive in an urban sea of humanity where sharks swarm and hooks are baited for suckers.

But there is one thing that Chip emphatically refuses to do.

He simply does not want to die—no matter how much someone seems to want him to. . . .

NO SCORE

NO SCORE

A Chip Harrison Novel

Lawrence Block

A SIGNET BOOK

SIGNET
Published by the Penguin Group
Penguin Books USA Inc., 375 Hudson Street,
New York, New York 10014, U.S.A.
Penguin Books Ltd, 27 Wrights Lane,
London W8 5TZ, England
Penguin Books Australia Ltd, Ringwood,
Victoria, Australia
Penguin Books Canada Ltd, 10 Alcorn Avenue,
Toronto, Ontario, Canada M4V 3B2
Penguin Books (N.Z.) Ltd, 182–190 Wairau Road,
Auckland 10, New Zealand

Penguin Books Ltd, Registered Offices:
Harmondsworth, Middlesex, England

Published by Signet, an imprint of Dutton Signet,
a division of Penguin Books USA Inc.

First Signet Printing, September, 1996
10 9 8 7 6 5 4 3 2 1

 REGISTERED TRADEMARK—MARCA REGISTRADA

Printed in the United States of America

PUBLISHER'S NOTE
This is a work of fiction. Names, characters, places, and incidents either are the product of the author's imagination or are used fictitiously, and any resemblance to actual persons, living or dead, events, or locales is entirely coincidental.

CHAPTER ONE

"I SHOULDN'T EVEN BE HERE," SHE SAID.

"Oh, you should," I said. I looked at her, and I got this very sudden, very tight feeling in my throat, as though I had done a very ungood job of swallowing something large. I swallowed again, and the tight feeling moved downward through my chest and stomach and down to the very pit of my stomach, where it settled and put down roots and applied for citizenship papers.

Now, you really must be cool, I told myself. Because she's here and so are you, and if you just Stay Cool and Play Your Cards Right everything will work out.

But the trouble with telling yourself things, I've discovered, is that the part of you that's being told is always dimly aware that the other part, the part that's doing the telling, is trying to *con* you, for Pete's sake. I mean, it's like staging a wrestling match between your two hands or trying to commit suicide by holding your breath. (If you try that, you eventually pass out and start right in breathing again. So I understand. I experimented once when I was about thirteen, but I got to thinking that maybe this was just a big story and you really could kill yourself that way if you were very strong-willed. And I decided that I was a pretty strong-willed person and was thus running a real risk, so what I did was go into this fake swoon and collapse gracefully on my bedroom rug. I was in my bedroom at the time, and all alone, so you might wonder why I didn't just start breathing more or less naturally instead of putting on an act. That would be a tough one to answer actually, but anyway none of this has very much to do with what was going on between me and Francine.)

What was going on between me and Francine was that we were in my room, not the bedroom where I held my breath and swooned but the room I was renting now, which was in an attic upstairs over a barbershop. Francine thought she shouldn't even be here, and I thought she should.

And I had this lump, or tightness really, in the pit of my stomach. Or, not to mince words, in my, well, groin.

"I should go home now," she said.

"You just got here."

"As soon as I finish this cigarette."

She took a puff on her cigarette and just let the smoke find its own way out of her mouth. She sat there on my bed with one hand on her lap and the other behind her on the bed and she let the smoke trickle out from between her lips, which were parted just enough to let this happen. The general effect was as though something was burning inside her. I could believe this.

I was on the bed next to her. That sounds sexier than it was. Because we were both sitting side by side on the edge of the bed, and we might as well have been sitting side by side on a bench, watching a basketball game, for Pete's sake. All it really was was uncomfortable.

Come on, I told myself. (Remember what I said about telling yourself things, about all the good it does.) Come on, *do* something. At least *say* something. Be masculine. Take the initiative. Act.

"You're beautiful," I said.

"Oh, come on."

"No, I really mean it. You are."

"Oh, sure," she said, but there was something going on in her eyes and around her mouth. She fluffed her hair with one hand. Her hair was the soft reddish brown of oak leaves just before they fall off the tree. I reached to touch her hair and she shook her head and I took my hand away. I did touch her hair more or less in passing. It was as soft as it looked.

She drew on the cigarette and let the smoke find its way to the ceiling again.

"That's easy to say, Chip," she said.

"No, I mean it."

"I'm sure you tell every girl."

"No."

"Well, how do you mean it?"

"Huh?"

She turned a little toward me, crossed one leg over the other (or perhaps it was the other way around). "Why do you say I'm beautiful?" she demanded. "I mean, what about me is that way?"

"Oh, well—"

"Just for the sake of conversation."

I gave a quick nod then, a reflexive gesture indicating that I had Gotten The Message. I remember reading somewhere that beautiful women are inclined to be very narcissistic, meaning that they are in love with themselves, and that the best way to have success with them is to let them know that you think they're every bit as great as they think they are. I read this in a book that told how to succeed with women, and that even gave little poetic lines to say to them at tender moments, but I had never bothered to commit any of the lines to memory because they struck me as fairly corny. Besides, it seemed to me that if the author was really such an expert at making out with women he would be too busy doing just that to waste his time writing books. Like the books that tell you how to make money at the racetrack, or how to turn a shoestring into a million dollars. If anybody could do those things, why bother writing a book? Why not just go ahead and do it?

"Your eyes," I said. Another book had suggested that every woman thinks her eyes are beautiful. "Brown eyes flecked with green, and so large, and so deep."

"Deep?"

"You think about things, Francine. You have deep and profound thoughts."

"That's very true."

"And it shows in your eyes."

"Honestly?"

"Honestly."

"So you like my eyes," she said, prompting.

And smiled a smile to let me know I was on the right track.

"And you have beautiful hands," I said.

"Do you think so?"

I reached out, trying not to let my own hand tremble, and I took hold of hers. She didn't draw away. This wasn't a pass, after all. It was part of the project of cataloguing Francine's charms. She made things easier by transferring her cigarette to her other hand, and I moved closer on the bed until I could feel the warmth of her body next to mine. We weren't exactly touching, but I could feel the warmth of her body.

I held her hand and told her how beautiful it was. As a matter of fact, it was a very fine hand, with just the right softness to it. The fingers were long and sensitive. There was just the finest tracing of soft downy hair on the back of the hand. And it had none of the faults that so many hands will have. It wasn't cold, it wasn't sweaty, it wasn't clammy. Of course, I didn't put things that way. I firmly believe in stressing the positive side of things. For the same reason I didn't mention the hand's one flaw, which was the nicotine stain between the first two fingers. I suppose I wouldn't have minded this if I smoked myself, but I didn't. I think it's a bad habit and I don't see any point in having bad habits. As a matter of fact, I do have one bad habit myself, but that stuff about it making you insane or blind is really a lot of nonsense, and anyway I've been doing my best to keep it to a rock-bottom minimum. And, of course, I intend to give it up as soon as I have a satisfactory substitute for it, which is what bringing Francine to my room was all about, actually, although from the way she had been acting you would have thought it was the furthest thing from her mind.

"And your hair," I said, reaching out to touch it. "And your tiny feminine feet, and your shapely legs—"

I went on like this. It was really pretty disgusting, when you come right down to it, but at the same time you have to realize that everything I said was the truth. Francine was so beautiful it could make your heart stop to look at her. A soft, beautiful, innocent face, and these gentle shoulders and slender arms, and her breasts—I still get weak in the knees just *thinking* about her breasts. You would think that breasts like those would be more at home on a heavier girl, but when your eyes moved down from those breasts (if in fact they did; mine often didn't, remaining there like two bees at two blossoms), you saw that the waist was very slim, and the hips just wide enough to be interesting, and the buttocks nicely rounded, and the legs as if they had stepped out of stocking ads. I could go on this way, but what's the point? Even if I pasted a photo of her right here, it wouldn't do it right, because all of us see things differently. So do this: Imagine an absolutely perfect girl (except for a nicotine stain between the first two fingers of the right hand, and a half-inch-long crescent-shaped scar on the inside of the left thigh) and you've imagined Francine.

I went on telling her this, leaving out those two flaws (only the first of which I knew about then) and wording my praise so that I cam of more like an artist and less like a total sex maniac, and all the while I kept looking at her eyes, and the weirdest thing happened. She began to get hypnotized.

I don't know what else you could call it. She was nodding encouragingly in time to the rhythm of my words, and every now and then she would chime in with *Do you really think so?* or *Do you honestly mean it?* or just a little *Yes* and *Uh-huh* and *Oh* sounds and grunts, and it was as if she was completely caught up in the sound of my voice telling her how perfect she was. I was pressing her hand as I talked and she was giving me little rhythmic squeezes in return.

You've got her, I thought. Now hurry, before the spell wears off.

But I guess I was afraid to blow it. Things were going so well, see, and I didn't want to jeopardize my position. Because it seemed as though I had been waiting forever for this to happen, and if it didn't happen soon I didn't know what I would do, except maybe go completely out of my head.

So I went on talking while the cigarette burned unattended between the fingers of her left hand— I was holding the right hand all the while. And very smoothly I went on talking and reached across and plucked the cigarette away and flipped it into the sink on the other side of the room. It was an easy shot because the other side of the room wasn't all that far away, the room being on the small side, but even so the whole maneuver was one of my smoother plays.

It encouraged me, and then, too, I realized that soon I was going to run out of parts of Francine to praise. So I got an arm around her and tipped up her face and kissed her.

At first it was like kissing—well, I was going to say a warm corpse, but that's really pretty revolting and it wasn't like that at all. Let's say it was like kissing someone who was asleep.

But then she started to wake up.

She kissed back, sort of tentatively, and I held her a little closer and kissed her a little more heavily, and she opened up like a flower. Her arms went around me and held me and her breasts pressed up against my chest and she sighed beautifully and her lips parted. There was a brief hissing sound as some drops from the leaky faucet put out her cigarette butt, and as the hissing died I let my tongue slip ever so gingerly past her lips and into the rich dark cave of her mouth.

She tasted of honey and tobacco and musk. She made the kiss a very urgent and hungry sort of experience, putting her own mouth into it and clutching my shoulders fiercely with her little hands.

First base, I thought.

I told myself to forget about the different bases, because that sort of thinking can be a trap. I had been to first base before, though not with Francine. I had been to second base a few times, and even to third base.

But, as you must have figured out by now, I had never been to home plate.

All right. Let's come right down and say it, let's put it down in black and white. I was a virgin.

What a stupid word.

I mean, it's a *girl's* word, right? Virgin, for Pete's

sake. You really can't come up with a more feminine word than virgin. You hear a word like that and you picture a girl with flowers in her hair, wearing something with ruffles. But I don't know of any other word for it, so that one will have to do. I, Chip Harrison, was a seventeen-year-old virgin. I wasn't going to be seventeen forever. (Although there were times when it seemed that way.) And I wasn't going to be a virgin forever, either, if I could help it. (Although there were times, damn it, when it didn't seem as though I could help it.)

As a matter of fact, it sort of seemed to me that the two things, age and sex, were connected in some heavy way. That if I scored (which is to say got to home plate, which is to say stopped being a virgin) before I turned eighteen, then I won. Whereas if I didn't, I lost.

But the point of all this is that the business with the bases can be a snare and a delusion, or at least I have found this to be so, because they give you the feeling that you are making progress with the girl, in that each time you are with her you get a little closer to the goal line (wrong sport, sorry about that) and thus it seems to follow that sooner or later you will score. This is not necessarily true. And, in fact, it seems that the more you get into this kind of pattern with a girl, the better she gets at getting you to stop somewhere along the way. It isn't that you keep getting closer but that you keep not getting where you wanted to go, and all of this is not only frustrating (very) but it leaves her knowing that she can control you, and this is not a Good Thing in any sense.

Not that I am the World's Foremost Authority on all this. To be honest, some of this I got from the books on how to succeed with women, and some is just speculation on my part. But what it all boils down to is that the best way to do something is to do it, and the best way to Go All The Way with a girl is to just go ahead and do it. Not in stages but all at once.

Especially because, in this particular instance, I was not going to get another chance at Francine. Because she was two years older than I was, and practically engaged to some college jerk, and so it had been a case of wild luck that I had gotten her to my room at all. So the chances were very good that I would never see her again, which was too bad, but which was something I could life with If Only. If only I hit the first pitch completely out of the park and ran around the bases and crossed the plate before Francine realized what had happened.

So we held the kiss, and she clung to me as

tightly as her sweater clung to her, and my tongue went spelunking in her mouth, and her tongue met it and got acquainted with it. We kissed for a long time. Then we came up for air and looked deep into each other's eyes, and when her eyes went slightly glassy I kissed her again, and it was the same, only better.

When we broke this time she said, "Oh, Chip—"

"Francine—"

"I must go."

"Francine—"

"Please, I can't—"

"You're so beautiful," I said, desperately.

"Oh, Chip."

"I love to kiss you."

"Oh."

"So beautiful. A goddess."

"Oh, my God—"

I drew her to me. She resisted, but not in any really meaningful way. She sort of stiffened, and I drew her close and got my mouth fastened to hers again, and then she got into the spirit of things again, as if the token show of resistance made it all right for her to surrender now. And in the course of drawing her close, somehow or other my hand managed to get on top of her breast.

Around first base and streaking for second.

* * *

Getting the sweater off was an absolute stone bitch. It really was. I guess because there is no entirely natural way to pull a tight yellow sweater over a girl's head. You can't just make believe it's happening by itself. It's possible to sort of slide into a kiss, or let your hands accidentally settle on the more interesting parts of a girl, but sweater removal is just too damned obvious. Even if you're both all in favor of it, it's hard to pretend you don't know what's going on. Or coming off, I suppose.

I got the sweater out of the waistband of her skirt without too much trouble. But then I started to work one hand up under the front of the sweater, and she broke the kiss and put her hand on mine, and pushed.

"Please, Chip."

"Francine, you're so beautiful."

"Chip, I don't want you to do that."

"I think you have the most beautiful breasts in the world."

"I don't—you do?"

"Yes."

"You're just saying that. Chip—"

A kiss, but not a very successful one.

"You have a great line, Chip. My goodness, what a line you have."

"It's not a line."

"Oh, your hands just won't behave. Please don't do that."

"Francine, I want to look at you."

"Oh, come off it. I know what you want."

"I have to see you."

"Sure, you just have to *see* me."

"Your breasts are beautiful, Francine."

"You shouldn't talk like that. I hardly know you. I mean, after all—"

"Beautiful."

"Oh."

"Beautiful."

"If I thought I could trust you—"

"You can trust me, Francine."

"I mean if it wasn't so utterly physical—"

"You know it's more than that, Francine."

"I mean—"

"Francine—"

"Oh," she said, finally, and shrugged me away, and just as I was about to reach for her again and start the whole process over, she gave a little sigh and pulled the sweater up over her head. There was a moment when the yellow sweater covered her head completely while leaving her chest uncovered (except for the bra, of course) and that image imprinted itself on my memory. There was something really appropriate about it, the whole image of Francine with the best part of her right out in the open and her stupid mouth covered up. If I were an artist I would paint that scene. I think if it was painted right you could look at it and know everything you would ever need to know about Francine.

But she was only like this for a second, and then the sweater was off and the arms were extended and the lips parted and the eyes glazed, and it was at that very moment that I knew for certain that I could forget about bases and goal lines and all, that I could stop crawling around inside my own head and giving myself halftime pep talks, because it was all set and all arranged and all decided and it was all in the bag and Chip Harrison was going to stop being a virgin and start being a man.

I kissed her.

And we stretched out on the bed together.

Her skin was so soft. It's unbelievable how soft girls are. I got my hands around her and unhooked her bra, and although I am not the deftest person on earth it went well enough, and I eased it off over her shoulders and bared her breasts. And just as I was doing this our eyes caught, and I looked at her eyes and her mouth, the whole expression on her face, and she was pleased and amused and calm, and her eyes said that she knew what was happening and liked what was happening and that everything would work out just fine.

She was so beautiful.

I got completely involved in those breasts. I couldn't stop touching and kissing them. It wasn't a question of trying to do one thing and then another, of trying to get further and further with her, because it had already been established that we were going to do the whole thing and all that mattered now was to do it as well as possible. So instead of trying to put something over on her, I was trying to excite her as much as possible and to do things that I enjoyed, and it sure worked.

"Oh, Chip. That feels so nice—"

Her skin tasted of sugar and spice and secret girls smells. I liked her breasts like a little kid with an ice-cream cone, wanting to take a big bite but wanting to make it last as long as I could. I nibbled and gobbled and she made these wonderful heavy breathing sounds and started squirming on the bed underneath me.

"Take off your shirt, Chip. I want to feel you against me."

When I take off my shirt, you don't get reminded at once of Greek sculpture. I'm not a ninety-seven-pound weakling, but I'm not exactly Charles Atlas either. I'm sort of bony and under-nourished in appearance. But I took the shirt off, and when I glanced at Francine's eyes, she didn't seem that disappointed with what I was unveiling. As a matter of fact, she looked hungry.

"Oh, Chip—"

I kissed her, and our tongues renewed their old friendship, and our chests pressed together. Mine got the better of the deal. Her nipples were as hard as little rosebuds and I brushed my upper body back and forth over them and she moaned and wiggled in response.

After a long time of kissing and touching and feeling, after I had told her how beautiful her breasts were and how delicious her flesh tasted and felt, and after she had told me how wonderful I made her feel and how sweet I was and how much she cared for me, after all of that, she lay down and closed her eyes and raised her hips a little so that I could take her skirt off. It wasn't hard at all. I just opened the button and unzipped the zipper and pulled the skirt down and off—it was a green plaid skirt, for those of you who don't have color sets. And then it was off, and she was lying there in her panties, and I discovered the half-inch crescent-shaped scar on the inside of her thigh, and I didn't think of it as a fault at all. In fact, I didn't think that Francine had any faults. Only good points, and an abundance of them.

I ran my hands over her legs. Until that moment I don't think I ever realized just how important legs are. Girls' legs, I mean. How important it is that they be great-looking. I had always paid a lot of attention to faces and breasts and behinds, and I knew the difference between great-looking legs and lousy-looking legs, but I was never that excited about legs.

You live and you learn. Francine had great-looking legs, and all spread out like that, naked except for the panties, I was really able to see the whole girl. As an entity, I mean. And I realized the importance of the legs.

(I don't know if this is coming through very well. Call it an intuitive flash, a sudden burst of insight, which after all is how most great discoveries come about. The major breakthroughs never occur because someone sat down and thought things out. They come in flashes. Newton and the apple, for instance. Paul on the road to Damascus. Archimedes in the bathtub. Chip Harrison in bed with Francine.)

"Chip?"

Her eyes were closed, and if there was any expression on her face, I couldn't read it. She seemed very calm, completely relaxed, but I could see she was trembling inside.

"You can take them off."

I put my hands on her shoulders. I ran them very slowly down over her breasts and stomach and grazed her panties and went on all the way down those legs to her feet.

"My panties. You can take them off."

"Yes."

"You can . . . do anything."

"Yes."

"Anything you want to."

Her voice was different than it had ever been before, older and younger, both at once. Softer, mostly. And as if for the first time, I was hearing Francine speak without any phoniness in the way.

I wanted to say something but I couldn't. My throat was blocked, knotted up.

I took off her pants. I took off her wispy nylon pants and squeezed them in a ball and held on to them with both hands. I wanted to nail them to the wall over the bed as a trophy. I wanted to sleep with them under my pillow. I wanted to chew them up and swallow them.

"Chip—"

I put the panties aside. I put my hands on her

thighs and she opened them, parted her thighs, and I looked at her.

I could smell her.

I put out a hand, touched her. She was moist. I put my finger into her just a little ways and I felt her. She was all wet and hot and sticky.

And it came to me, all at once, that this was not just a dumb girl with a great body that I was going to ball. It came to me that she was far more than this. It came to me, as I crouched over her with my finger inside her, that I loved this girl. And that she was what I had been looking for, a beautiful, passionate woman whom I could love and honor and cherish forever.

But first, by God, I was going to ball her.

I played with her with both hands. I played with her, absolutely delighted with the way she was built and the way she felt and the effect it was all having on her. And she lay there, hips rolling so nicely, so sweetly, so gracefully, and she kept her eyes closed and her hands at her sides, and the words flowed in a stream.

"Oh Chip, it's so good, it's so good, I like it, I love it, it's so good. I'm so hot, I like it, I love it, Chip, it's so good—"

I fingered her with one hand and attacked my own clothes with the other. To do this properly probably takes great skill and coordination, like rubbing your tummy while you pat your head. I tugged on my belt to unhook it and I pulled so hard I very nearly strangled myself at the waist. But I did get my pants down, and wriggled until they were off, and my shorts as well. I had kicked off my shoes some time ago. I never did get my socks off. I might have taken the trouble, but while I was getting the shorts off my other hand slipped a little, and without really planning it that way I discovered Francine's clitoris.

(I hadn't planned on mentioning that. After all, it's pretty clinical, and maybe not in the best of taste to come right out and talk about something like a clitoris. Not that there's anything wrong with a clitoris, for Pete's sake. But that there might be something wrong with mentioning it. But the thing of it is, I had known about this part of a girl from my reading, and knew of the great importance of it, but had somehow not gotten around to looking for it, being so preoccupied with other goodies. But now just by accident I had found it, and a good thing it was.)

"Oh, wow! Oh, God, yes! Oh, Jesus Christ, do it! Oh, do it forever!"

I got on top of her. I kept touching her, and I got on top of her, and I thought that this was it, this was really it. I was still seventeen and in a second I would stop being a virgin, which was a damned good thing, because if you were old enough to fight for your country you were certainly old enough to have sex, and with a sexual revolution going on, the idea of an eighteen-year-old male virgin was pretty ridiculous, and here I was, getting ready not to be one anymore, and here Francine was, all wet and open and ready, and I loved her, by God, and I would love her forever, and wasn't I the lucky son of a gun?

I said, "I love you, Francine."

"Do it!"

"I love you."

"God, God, stick it in!"

And it occurred to me, albeit briefly, that this might be a kind of graphic thing for a girl to say, and maybe not in the best of taste, but then I decided that it was all to the good, that Francine was, after all, carried away in the throes of passion, and that it was a fine sign that a girl like Francine, so demure on the outside, could be so carried away by passion, and then I stopped thinking entirely, and readied myself for the move that would change my life once and forever, and stabbed blindly ahead, and missed, and took aim again, and—

And paused, because it seemed that a herd of elephants was stampeding up the staircase and down the hall, and voices were shouting, and Francine was roaring at me, begging me to do it, to stick it in, and I lay there, paralyzed, and the door to my room exploded inward, and a man the size of a mountain charged inside. He had a hand the size of a leg of lamb, and in that hand he had a gun the size of a cannon.

"You son of a bitch!" he bellowed.

And pointed the gun at me, and pulled the trigger.

CHAPTER TWO

I SUPPOSE YOU'RE WONDERING JUST WHO I am, anyway, and how I got myself into this particular mess. At least I *hope* you're wondering something along those lines, because if you're not, it means that you aren't interested, which in turn would mean that I have failed to hook your interest and rivet your attention in the preceding pages. And if I fail to get high marks in hooking and riveting, I probably won't be able to sell this book when I'm done writing it, and then I don't know what I'll do. For the past two weeks I've been living in a room about the size of a midget's footlocker and eating Maine sardines and stale bread. The sardines are seventeen cents a can and the bread is free, but even if they were both free they would not be all that much of a bargain, because a sardine sandwich, even when you haven't had one in a while, is not exactly a dish to set before a king, and when the sardines are the cheapest ones available and the bread is stale and the menu never changes, well, I'm not fussy about food, but I can think of things I'd rather have.

I'm sorry. I'm getting completely off the track. The point is that the last chapter was supposed to hook and rivet you. And now that I've got your attention (if I haven't lost it already by wandering off the subject), I really ought to tell you who I am and how all this happened.

My name is Chip Harrison. It wasn't always, although I was always called Chip, as what you might call a nickname, because when I was a little tyke my first word was something that sounded like *Tsib*. (God only knows what I was trying to say. *Mama*, probably.) Anyway, *Tsib* wasn't anybody's idea of a terrific name for a kid, but *Chip* was pretty good, as in *Chip Off The Old Block*. So I got called that a lot.

Then in late 1963 I started getting called that exclusively, and my actual name began not being entered on school records and things like that. Because my name, you see, was a combination of family names. Leigh, which was my mother's maiden name, and Harvey, which was my father's mother's maiden name. So that my name started out as Leigh Harvey Harrison, and ever since late 1963 people named Leigh Harvey Anything have been very willing to be called something else.

"The sheerest coincidence," my father told my mother. "The sheerest possible coincidence. But when there are enough people in the world, coincidences have to happen now and again. I went to school with a Jewish lad named Adolph Gittler. His parents named him this in all innocence, you know, never dreaming—well, the point is clear. The boy changed his name to Arnold Gidding. Didn't do him all that much good. The teachers called him Arnold, but we all called him Adolph. Or Der Fuehrer. Or Sieg Heil."

"Boys are so cruel," my mother said.

"Leigh Harvey," my father said. "A perfectly sound name turned frightful overnight. We'll change it to Chip. That's what everyone calls him anyway. Chances are no one really knows his full name. When he gets older, why, if he wants something more distinguished, he can select it himself."

If I ever do, I suppose I will.

* * *

I wasted all of yesterday writing out the story of my childhood, and where I was born and where we lived while I was growing up and the schools I went to and things like that, and I used up a whole lot of time and paper, and I just got through tearing it all up. Because in the first place I can't imagine anyone being very interested in all of that, since there was nothing the least bit unusual or attention-grabbing about it. And in the second place I'm not one of these people who can practically remember emerging from the womb. I have partial recall, and it's vague at best.

So why don't I just say that I came of rich but dishonest parents, and went to a couple of different private boarding schools, until that one jarring day when my father shot my mother in the back of the head and shot himself in the front of the head and made me, in the wink of an eye, an orphan.

I was playing basketball when I learned this. I'm fairly tall, which always leads people to think that I ought to be good at basketball, until they come to the realization that my lack of coordination offsets my height, since I'm not Gulliver or anything, just fairly tall for my age. This particular coach hadn't caught on yet, it being my first year at this particular prep school, so I was out there on the court missing layups and muffing rebounds when some kid came down with a note asking me to report to the Head's office.

The Head—he was always called this, and while this is true of a lot of headmasters, it really fit in his case, because he had a head the approximate size of a basketball, perched on a skinny neck above an insignificant body, the head itself as hairy as a doorknob, with vague indentations and protrusions here and there to indicate eyes and nose and mouth and all that. Anyway, the Head did a lot of pacing around his office that day, and told me what had happened, more or less, and then went on to tell me more or less why my father had done this unprecedented thing.

What it amounted to, without the hemming and hawing that the Head put in, was that Chip Harrison's parents had spent their lives as con men (well, con man and con wife) and had made a good if shaky living for many years, working one swindle or another, and had been in the process recently of pulling off a remarkable stock swindle, until suddenly the roof had fallen in, leaving my unpoor but unhonest parents (a) stone broke and (b) jailable. Evidently my father decided that there was No Way Out, whereupon he did what he did.

I can't understand why. I mean, it seems to me that there must have been something he could have done. Gone to Brazil or joined the Foreign Legion or something. But I guess he just had the feeling that all the walls and the ceiling were coming in on him, and it seemed simpler to go bang bang and end it.

"I never knew him," I said, dazed. "I was never around much, and then when I wasn't at some school or other, well, I was usually off at summer camp, or else I was with them and we were traveling. They always seemed to be moving to one place or another."

"One step ahead of the law," the Head said darkly.

"Uh, I suppose. I guess I never really knew what he did for a living. When kids would ask, I would say he was in investments. I thought he probably was, but I didn't have any clear idea of how."

"Rather shady investments," said the Head.

"I don't suppose I thought about it too much. I took it for granted, ever since I was old enough to think about it, because little kids don't think about the subject, or at least I didn't until recently—"

"Would you like a glass of water, Harrison?"

"I don't think so. What I mean is, I took it for granted we were rich. We always had everything, and then being at schools like this one, I just thought we were rich."

"Ah, yes, errmphhh," the Head said. "That does, errmphhh, bring up a painful subject, Harrison."

"It does?"

It did. The subject was money, and the pain lay in the fact that I didn't have any. I wasn't just an orphan. I was a penniless orphan, a seventeen-year-old Oliver Twist. If my parents had seemed to be rich, they had managed this illusion by spending every ill-gotten penny as soon as they ill-got their hands on it. And over the past months they had been spending a great deal of money that they didn't have yet, all of this snowballing up to the point when everything went blooey, so that not only did I have an inheritance of absolutely nothing coming to me, but I was in hock to the Upper Valley Preparatory Academy for a couple thousand dollars' worth of tuition and room and board.

"I'm sure you understand the problem, Harrison," the Head said. The light glinted off the shiny top of the Head's head. He picked up one object after another from his desktop—a pipe, a pipe cleaner, a pencil, an ashtray, a file folder, you name it. He played with each of these things, and he watched himself do this, and I watched him, and it went on like this for a while.

Then he told me I would have to make arrangements, find relatives who would take me in and help me carve out a fresh start in life for myself. Perhaps, he suggested, someone might come to my financial assistance. I told him that as far as I knew, I didn't have any relatives. He acknowledged that he had rather thought this might be the case.

"I really don't know what I'll do after graduation," I said. "I guess college is out, at least for the time being, not that any of them have been in what you might call a rush to accept me, but—"

I got a look at his face and it put me off-stride. I let the sentence die and waited.

I'm afraid you don't entirely understand," he said. "I don't see how we could conscientiously let you remain here until graduation, Harrison. You see—"

"But it's February."

"Yes."

"Almost March."

"Errmphhh."

"I mean, this is my last semester before graduation. I would be graduating in June."

"Actually, you owe us tuition, room, and board since September, Harrison."

"I'll pay sooner or later. I'd go to work after graduation and I could pay—"

He was shaking his head, which in his case called for more than the usual amount of effort. I watched him do this. I felt, oh, very strange. Weird. I mean, thinking about all of this now, in what you might call historical perspective, I get all sorts of vibrations that I didn't get then. Like what an utter shit, pardon the expression, the Head was. And like that.

But at the time, I was having my whole little world turned not only upside down but inside out, and I was like numb. I didn't know how I felt about any of this because I didn't *feel*. I couldn't. There was no time to react because everything was too busy going on.

The Head stopped shaking and spoke again. "No, no, no," it—*he*—said. "No, I think not. No, I'm afraid we'll simply have to write off the money, chalk it up to experience. If there were mitigating circumstances, but no, no, no, I don't think so. Your grades are not bad, but neither are they exceptionally good. Coach Lipscot tells me your performance on the basketball court is generally disappointing. And, of course, the social stigma, you must understand. Murder and suicide and confidence swindling, no, no, no, I think not, Harrison, I think not."

* * *

I was shaking when I left his office. I don't think I was ticked off or scared or any particular thing, but I was shaking. Everything happening at once. I went back to the dorm. My roommate was lying in his bunk, reading a sex magazine, and when I walked in he went through his little act of trying to pretend that (a) he was only interested from the standpoint of a future psychologist and (b) he had been holding the magazine in both hands. I don't suppose the guy beat off more than average. It was his attitude that bothered me. (As a matter of fact, an obnoxious attitude in this area isn't exactly rare. Either they're like Haskell, going to great lengths to pretend that they don't even have genitals, let alone touch them, or else they go to the other extreme and want to talk about it, or discuss methods, or do it right out in the open. Or worse. Either way I find it pretty disgusting. I think it should be a private thing, like religion or squeezing blackheads.)

Anyway, the sight of old Haskell draping the sex book to hide his erection was enough to turn me off to the idea of talking with him, which hadn't been that outstanding an idea to begin with, I don't guess. He started babbling about something or other, and I wondered what he would say if I told him everything, and I decided it wasn't worth finding out. I turned away from him and went over to my dresser and started pulling out drawers. I thought I was trying to decide what to take and what to leave, but I guess I was looking for something without knowing what it was, something that would make everything go together in some, oh, meaningful way. If anything like that existed, it certainly wasn't in my drawers or closet. As a matter of fact, the more I looked the more I realized that there was nothing around that I particularly wanted to see again. It was just too much trouble to decide which stuff to put in a suitcase and which stuff to leave behind.. It was easier to leave everything.

It was especially easy to leave old Haskell. I didn't even say good-bye. I mean, why do it? I thought about borrowing a few bucks from him— he always had plenty of money; everybody at Upper Valley always had money. The Head would just shake himself and say that he had expected me to borrow money before I left, and like father like son, and all of that.

So I didn't. Not from Haskell and not from anybody else, and the crazy thing is that if I had just gone and told people what was happening, not even getting specific about it but just that I was broke and with nowhere to turn and all, I could have collected a bundle. Not by borrowing, but as outright gifts, or on a pay-me-when-you-can basis. Because while the guys at Upper Valley were something less than princes, they were not a bad bunch. And if I was not Mr. Popularity, I wasn't anybody they despised, either. They were okay, and I got along with everybody. And, more than anything else, see, these guys were all at Upper Valley for a reason. They were all there because (a) they had money and (b) there was something less than wonderful about them, or else they would have gone to a better school. Either they were slow learners or marginal alcoholics or their family background had a bad smell to it or something of the sort. They had plenty of money and they knew how important money was and just what the limits to it were, and all of this added up to a gentle and wry kind of sympathy and all.

So they might even have taken up a collection for me, and it might even have come to enough so that I could have stayed at that crappy school until I graduated from it. At least it would have ben enough to let me leave the school on a bus or train or something.

But I was, well, proud. And in no mood to explain anything to anybody, or take anything from anybody. In fact I couldn't even talk to anybody, although I had this need. I actually spent close to two hours just walking around the campus, trying to think who I could talk to. I couldn't work up any enthusiasm for talking to any of the guys or any of the teachers. I would have little conversations with some of them in my own mind, and it helped me get some of my own thoughts straightened out, but each time I came to the decision that I would just as soon talk to these people in my mind and not in the flesh. And I certainly didn't want to talk to the basketball coach. I did have an imaginary conversation with him. It didn't get too far, but it featured him explaining to me how, if I only drove more fiercely on those lay-ups and worked harder for those rebounds, if I could only be counted on to drop a sufficient percentage of foul shots, then my academic career might still be promising. "You've got the height and the reach, Chip, kid," he said, in the privacy of my mind. "Not enough to interest the college scouts. A year or two and the rest of them'll catch up with you. But on a prep school level—well, you had your chance, boy. This was the place for you and I gave you every opportunity, but you just didn't give me everything, boy; you just let me and the team down. A winner never quits, Chip, kid, and a quitter never wins."

I sat under a tree and looked through my wallet. I had a snapshot of my folks, and another more formal picture of my mother. I looked at these for a little while. I also had seven one-dollar bills in the bill compartment of the wallet, and forty-six cents in the change compartment. In the secret compartment I had a folded twenty-dollar bill and a lubricated Trojan with a receptacle tip. The two were related; I had planned, at some unspecified future date, to hitchhike to the city fifty miles away where, it was said, prostitutes plied their hoary trade. The twenty-dollar bill was to hire one, and the Trojan was to make sure that any scars left by the experience would be psychological in type. And the secret compartment, by the way, was not all that much of a secret. I had been carrying that stupid rubber for so long that you could see its elliptical outline through the wallet.

(I guess it worked, though. Not the secret compartment. The Trojan. In all the time I had it there, I never once caught a disease.)

I got up from under the tree and put the wallet back in my pocket. I had $27.46 and an old rubber. I had no place to go to and no one to turn to and I couldn't even stay where I was.

I went back to my room. Haskell, thank God, was not there. I think he was probably having dinner. It was about that time, and I could have gone over and had something myself, but I didn't even consider it. I got under the shower and washed myself a few times, and I got dressed in all clean clothes, and I brushed my teeth and combed my hair and made polishing motions at my shoes. I put things like my comb and toothbrush and a bar of soap in my pockets. I thought about packing a change of socks and underwear, but I didn't. I wanted to have my hands free. The phrase *walking away empty-handed* came to me, and it seemed proper to do this, and in a literal sense.

On the highway, neatly groomed and clean cut, I stood with my thumb in the air. A few cars came and went, as cars will do, and then a big Lincoln slowed down, and I got that good expectant feeling, and I straightened up a little and put a fresh, boyish smile on my face.

The car slowed a little more, and the driver looked at me, and stepped down hard on the gas pedal and roared off into the distance.

All I could think of was a joke. You probably know it. I guess it's the oldest joke in the world.

There was this guy who joined the paratroops, and after all the training it was time for him to make his first actual jump from a plane. Not off one of the towers but out of an actual plane in flight. And the flight instructor or jump instructor or whatever they call it, the guy in charge, went through the procedure with him. "When you jump, you count to ten. Then you pull the ripcord to open the chute. In the event that the chute does not open, pull the emergency cord to open the parachute. The chute will open and you will coast gently down to the ground. There a truck will pick you up and take you back to the base."

So the guy jumped, and he pulled the ripcord, and nothing happened, and he pulled the other cord, and nothing happened. And he said to himself, "I'll bet that fucking truck won't be there either."

Oldest joke in the world.

And I just fell out. I broke up completely. I rolled around at the side of the road, laughing harder than I ever laughed in my life. "That fucking truck," I said, and roared with laughter. "That fucking truck."

I never did cry. I don't know why, but I never did. And if I didn't that day, I don't suppose I ever will.

The car that picked me up, long after the laughter was over and done with, was a big Pontiac convertible with deep vinyl seats and power everything. The driver was about forty or forty-five, very pale and indoors-looking. He said he was a salesman and that he sold industrial bathroom fixtures. My first reaction was to wonder what an industrial bathroom was, and after I figured it out without asking him, I got a mental picture of an endless row of urinals stretching as far as the eye could see, with an endless row of workers in denim overalls, stepping up to the urinals, setting down their lunchboxes, and urinating industriously.

And it struck me that I had done this myself maybe a million times, except for the lunchbox and the overalls but in all those times it hadn't occurred to me that there were people who made a living going around selling urinals, or that other people made their living buying them. I had just never really given much thought to the way people made their livings. But now, as an orphan with twenty-seven dollars and change, the whole subject of work seemed more significant.

I found about a thousand questions to ask him. About the different models of industrial bathroom fixtures, and the colors they came in, and how you got into that kind of business, and, oh, everything that came to me. Now and then I would see him giving me funny little looks, as if he maybe thought I was putting him on by pretending to be interested in such a ridiculous subject. But I guess it was easier for him to believe that I was interested than to accept the fact that his work was all that boring, so he told me a lot more about his field than anyone in or out of it would really care to know. And he got a kick out of it, I guess, maybe because no one else thought he was so interesting. His wife, he told me at one point, didn't give a whoop in hell about his life's work. In fact, he said, she seemed ashamed of it, as though there was something dirty about sinks and toilets and urinals, when, in point of fact, the world would be infinitely filthier without them.

I wasn't faking a thing. I was really interested at the time. Honestly.

He picked me up in western Pennsylvania, where the school was. We took the Pennsylvania Turnpike west. It turned into the Ohio Turnpike, and we went about halfway through Ohio before he had to turn off. He left me on the pike. I had said I was going to Chicago, and while I didn't have a great reason to go there, I was stuck with the story.

Before he left me off, he stopped for gas and bought me a meal at the restaurant. He went to the john, and when he got back to the table, he was all excited and took me back to the john to show me all the plumbing fixtures and explain various things about them. We got some very funny looks from the others, let me tell you.

Through Ohio and Indiana and Illinois I talked to a lot of different people and had a total of six more rides. The conversations were something like the one I'd had with the salesman. I won't bore you with what the various drivers did for a living or where they picked me up and dropped me off, or the makes of the cars and appearance of the drivers. To tell you the truth, I don't remember it all that clearly. They tend to run together in my mind. Anyway, none of it was that sensational.

I got to Chicago a little before noon. My last driver dropped me north of town near the lake, and I spent almost an hour trying to hitch a ride back toward the center of the city. I suppose it must have been a whole lot less than an hour. In that wind, though, it seemed like forever. Finally a cop car came along and a uniformed cop stuck his head out and said something about hitchhiking. I didn't catch the words, but it didn't take an IQ up around the genius level to get the message, which was that hitchhiking was frowned upon. If he hadn't told me this, I might still be there, frozen solid, with my thumb out.

Now, though, it occurred to me to take a bus, which cost me a quarter and which was the first expenditure I'd had since I left school.

Sitting on that bus, all I could think of was the damned quarter. I mean, after all, I had gone something like twelve hundred miles and eaten three times and all I was out so far was a quarter. You'd think I would be thrilled, for Pete's sake. But I kept thinking that my $27.46 was now down to $27.21. And that I could afford to take the bus a hundred and eight more times, and then I'd have twenty-one cents left, which would buy me two cups of coffee and a gumball. The point being that I had no money coming in, so *any* going out was something to worry about.

I kept planning to ask the driver to let me out when we got to the center of town, but I couldn't think of a way to do this without sounding like a hopeless hick, and for some stupid reason I didn't want to. So I just kept looking around and waiting. I had been to Chicago before with my parents but couldn't remember much about it. Except that we went shopping at Marshall Field's and stayed, I think, at the Palmer House—though when I went to take a look at it, I didn't notice anything familiar about it. I guess I must have been eight or ten at the time.

Anyway, I recognized the Loop when we first hit it, and when we got to State Street, I remembered that it was the main drag, or else I just recognized it from the song. The street signs have *State Street* and under it *That Great Street*. When I noticed this I was tremendously pleased. A point of recognition, as if the street sign was some old school buddy or something. Later, after I had walked all over the damned street, I began to realize how incredibly simple it was of them to put something like that on the dippy street signs. If everybody who goes to Chicago could just see one of those signs once, that would be fine. But to just have them there always, so that even the people who live there have to look at them— .

I got off the bus at State Street and started walking around. I mostly stayed right there on That Great Street because it was a nice familiar name and if I left it I was afraid I might never find it again. I walked up and down and looked in store windows at things I didn't need and couldn't buy anyway. I kept seeing things that for no reason at all I suddenly wanted. A combination nail clipper and pocket knife, for example, which I needed like the Venus de Milo needs gloves. And although a guy had bought me breakfast just a couple of hours before, I kept getting these dumb yens for food. I couldn't pass any place that sold anything edible without starting to drool. I stood in front of a restaurant where the cheapest dish on the menu was over four dollars, and I actually stood there reading the whole menu as if I could go in there and dive into a steak. I mean, even if I was fool enough to waste the money, I wasn't dressed for the place.

Eventually I got annoyed and bought a candy bar just to kill my appetite. They had the nerve to charge six cents for a stinking nickel candy bar.

$27.15.

Two hours later I was stretched out on a bed in a room in the Eagle Hotel (*$3.50 a night*), reading the want-ad section of the *Chicago Tribune* (*free, out of a trash can*). I used a yellow chewed-up pencil stub (*found at the curb*) to mark the ads that looked promising.

There were jobs all over the place. Just looking at those listings, you wouldn't believe there was anyone in the country who wasn't working. The only problem was that none of the advertisers wanted to hire a seventeen-year-old kid with three and a half years of high school, no experience whatsoever, and not an awful lot of ability, either.

Not that they seemed to care too much about ability. The main thing seemed to be experience. I would say that ninety-eight ads out of a hundred wanted to hire people with experience, and what they were really hot to hire was someone who was already doing a much more important job at higher pay in the same field. I didn't blame them, but how could anybody get experience if you had to have it to get a job?

Another thing you had to have was an education. Judging by the ads, if the job was one where you might come up once a week against a two-syllable word, they wouldn't touch you unless you had a college degree, and they wouldn't be happy about it unless you had a master's. For less intellectual jobs, like picking ticks off horses, they were willing to settle for you if you had a high school diploma.

It was very goddamned discouraging, let me tell you. I folded the paper and put it down and sat up on the bed—$3.50 a night doesn't buy you much of a bed, incidentally—and said, aloud, "I'll bet that fucking truck won't be there, either."

This time it didn't break me up in the slightest. I went back to the paper and kept finding the two percent of the ads that I almost qualified for. Things like passing out handbills on the street, sweeping the floor in a grocery store, jobs that were either temporary or part-time and that didn't pay all that well anyway.

When I was done, I stretched out on the bed and closed my eyes. The hotel must have been made out of secondhand egg cartons. You could hear absolutely everything, Whenever a toilet flushed anywhere in the building, it was like being next to Niagara Falls. Sometimes I could hear conversations, either two people talking together just low enough so that I could make out every fifth word, or else some drunk shouting at the top of his lungs. I don't know which was worse.

But lying there I realized what I was going to do.

I was going to Succeed.

Of course you can't just succeed. You have to succeed *at* something, and I wasn't quite sure what that something might be yet. But the impression I got from the men I hitchhiked with was that one job wasn't all that different from any other. Once you got past the slave level and actually got somewhere in business, the idea was to take something and sell it to someone else. And it didn't really make very much difference whether the thing you were selling was advertising space or snake oil or industrial bathroom fixtures. The object, whatever it was, was to wind up with more money than you started out with.

I sat up in bed. I thought of my father and mother, and the life they had led, and where it in turn had led them. I would arrange my life differently. I would be honest and hard-working and stable. I would take as my own personal day-to-day objective the same goal that made all those hitchhikers the same—to finish each day with more money than I'd started the day with. If I had to pass out handbills or sweep floors or pick ticks off horses, I would do it for the time being, and I would make damn well sure that each day's work brought me at least as much as I needed for my meals and rent.

And meanwhile I would find some job that had some kind of real Opportunity For Advancement. That was a phrase that appeared in a great many ads, and they couldn't all be playing games. I'd find a job with an Opportunity For Advancement, and I would work long hours and apply myself and go to night school to get that high school diploma and then go on to take night courses at college and put myself through college, and work my way up the corporate ladder in the good old

American way, using hard work and pluck and luck and good old common sense and elbow grease to make my way to the top.

And there would be women every step of the way.

My brain spun at the thought. Of course there would be women, I realized. The cheap-but-vital women in whose rough arms I would learn the rudiments of love. The secretaries and career girls with whom I would share idle moments of brief but intense pleasure. And, when I found her, the Right Girl who would share my hopes and dreams, and with whom I would climb the long ladder rung by rung and hand in hand, until together we would enjoy the fruits of success crowned by True Love.

I thought of the joys of True Love, and glowed at the thought. And then I thought of the Untrue Love that would come first, with the career girls and secretaries and cheap-but-vital women, and I began to be moved by these thoughts. The thoughts became quite vivid, as a matter of fact, and quite moving.

But then someone in a room down the hall was seized by a coughing and spitting fit, and that ruined the mood completely.

I burrowed under the covers. A cockroach scuttled out from beneath the radiator, which had begun clanking. It seemed to be giving off a whole lot more noise than heat. The radiator, that is. Not the cockroach. Well, maybe the cockroach too, for all I knew. Or cared.

I settled my head on the pillow, such as it was. If there were more than thirty-five feathers in that pillow, they must have been very small ones. The man with tuberculosis (my diagnosis) did his number again.

I fell asleep. Which should give you an idea how tired I was.

CHAPTER THREE

THE MAN WAS MOSTLY SHOULDERS. HE wasn't really big, I was taller than he was, but he had these wide shoulders and no neck at all, and he was wearing a sinister short-brimmed hat and a black suit, and he looked like a Chicago gangster. Maybe he was nothing more desperate than a Chicago mutual funds salesman, but I don't really think so. I think he was a Chicago gangster. If not, he's in the wrong line of work.

In which case I know exactly how he feels.

He came toward me, and I picked up the rhythm of his walk and got my timing into gear. When he was just the right distance away, I took the pasteboard slip from the top of the stack and thrust it at him. If it had been a knife, and a couple of inches longer, it would have pierced his left lung.

But it was just a piece of paper and it never touched him. And amazingly enough he never touched it, either. He just kept right on walking and went past me as if I were invisible. I turned to look after him.

"Stay awake, Chip!"

I spun around. Gregor clicked the shutter, and I opened my hand and let the piece of pasteboard float to the ground. My gangster friend had missed his golden opportunity, all spelled out in smudged black letters on a yellow card, and saying:

HELLO THERE!

Your candid photo has just been taken by Gregor the Pavement Photographer! Your picture will be ready within twenty-four hours! Bring or mail this card with the some of one ($1.00) dollar to Gregor the Pavement Photographer, 1104 Halstead! Find out what you look like to others! See yourself as the world sees you!

It was a pretty tacky little slinger, no question about it. And even if you dropped the excess exclamation points and spelled *sum* right and printed the message in unsmudged ink on a less gaudy stock, it would still be nothing that most people would want to carry with them forever. That few of them were so moved was readily seen by a glance at the pavement to my rear, where any number of the yellow cards presently reposed.

In plain English, there were little yellow slingers all over the place, some of them crumpled, others just plain dropped. Most people dropped them without even finding out what they were, but almost all of them did take the cards when I shoved them at them. The gangster was rare. The average person has trouble not taking anything you hand him. It's a reflex, I suppose. I don't know whether the gangster had lousy reflexes or tremendous cool, or whether he was so tied up in his own little world that he hadn't even seen me. Nor did I have time to worry about this, because I had to pass the next card to the next person, who would in due course add it to Chicago's littering problem.

The gangster came by around a quarter after four, and there wasn't another memorable person for the rest of the day. This was my sixth day working for Gregor, and by now a person had to be pretty remarkable in order for me to take any real notice of him. Every day I would see tens of thousands of people, and I would poke yellow slips at thousands of people, and I would poke yellow slips at thousands of them. At first it was such a constant parade of new faces and bodies that I started getting a headache from it. But then it straightened out and smoothed out and the pedestrians lost their individuality. They were just part of the crowd, and I found myself tuning them out the way you tune out anything that's always there. I no longer really noticed the traffic noises, and I no longer smelled the smell of State Street, and in the same kind of way I no longer noticed the swarm of people. Every once in a while one of them would manage to be more than just another shadow in the crowd. The gangster type, and an occasional cripple, and particularly attractive girls, for example.

A few minutes after six, Gregor said, "Oh, the hell with it, keed, let's call it a day." He folded up his tripod and put his camera in the case. We walked to 1104 Halstead Street, where Co-op Photography was located. Co-op Photography was a name to put on the door, actually. Inside the door there was a large room jammed with desks and three smaller rooms, two of them darkrooms and one of them a slapdash studio with lights and a couple of backdrops. For ten dollars a month Gregor got the use of a desk, two hours a day of darkroom time, and use of the studio by arrangement. There was also a switchboard and a girl who functioned as a sort of collective receptionist, but it cost an extra five dollars a month to receive calls there, and Gregor figured it wasn't worth it. So we walked past the girl without asking if anyone had called, and Gregor put some things in the desk and took some other things out of it, one of them being a bottle of peach-flavored brandy.

"Jesus sonofabitching Christ," he said, reflectively. Gregor was a short dark mixture of various Balkan strains that didn't go together all that well. His eyes were sunken and his cheeks hollow. He had the heaviest beard of anyone I ever met. When he swore I always had the feeling I was hearing wrong, because he never sounded mad or aggravated or anything. He would say various obscene things in the tone of voice you would use to say, "I'm going down to the store for a new tube of toothpaste" or "I wonder how the White Sox did today." It took a whole lot of getting used to.

He uncapped the bottle and took a drink and asked me if I wanted one. I said it sounded like a good idea. He gave me the bottle and I took a drink. The first time he had done this I wanted to wipe the neck of the bottle or something, but then

I decided that anybody who stood out in the middle of State Street all day the way I had done was already exposed to every germ known to modern man, and besides there was something vaguely insulting about insinuating that Gregor was diseased or something.

I don't know what good peach-flavored brandy tastes like, or even if there is any such thing, for Pete's sake. This was very cheap stuff. If you've never had it, you've got the right idea. I think you could duplicate the taste by mixing equal parts of the sweet syrup from canned peaches and Zippo lighter fluid, but if you mixed it that way it would probably cost you more than Gregor paid for it.

He took another drink himself and put the cap on the bottle and the bottle in the drawer. Another photographer, an old man who wore suspenders all the time, believe it or not, came over and asked how it had gone.

"How should it go?" Gregor demanded. "You take the pictures and you see what happens." He pawed through a handful of letters on the desktop, held one of them to the light, and squinted suspiciously at it. "So either there's a dollar in it or there isn't," he said thoughtfully. "And what difference does it make?"

You may have gathered that he didn't have the

greatest money-making operation in the world. Good gathering. Gregor, from what I had seen, was a pretty fair photographer, but one look around that office told you that pretty fair photographers were in less demand than, say, pretty fair aerospace engineers. (Whatever they are: I don't understand the term, but the *Tribune*'s classified pages are filled with people who want to hire them.)

Gregor's business was straightforward enough. He stood there on State Street, taking pictures of people walking by, and as they passed I gave them a numbered slip, and theoretically they sent in the slip with a dollar, and theoretically the number on the slip enabled Gregor to find the right negative and print it and send the print to the customer.

"I don't always get the right picture to the right person," he had confided once. "Especially before I started using a kid. I would do the shooting and the card-passing all by myself, and I would get the numbers a little off-synch, and then I'd get some jerk writing in from Denver to tell me that he got the wrong picture, and I should either send him the right one or send his dollar back. So how am I supposed to straighten it out? Some of the jerks write back three, four times for a lousy dollar. Think how many times I must make a mistake and they don't write at all. Sometimes I wonder if anybody ever gets the right picture. But what do they want it for in the first place, huh, keed? Answer me that. I have this way of making a buck and I am damned if I can tell you why anybody at all ever sends for the Jesus sonofabitching Christ photographs."

Tonight his mood was less reflective. He seemed annoyed at the volume of late mail, and he cursed pleasantly as he slit the flaps of the envelopes and shook out the dollar bills. There were a couple of checks, and one clown had sent a dollar in stamps, and another hadn't enclosed any payment at all.

He put away the orders he would fill tomorrow and added the money to his wallet. "The one with the stamps," he said, "should sit on a hot stove waiting for his picture to come, the son of a bitch. Let's see, keed, eleven-thirty to five-thirty is six hours at a buck and a half is what? Nine bucks?"

"Eleven to six. Seven hours."

"Ten bucks?"

"Ten-fifty."

He counted out ten singles. He didn't have any change, he said. I had change, I said. So he discovered two quarters in his pocket and gave them to me.

"You're the only one making any money," he

told me. "Don't spend it all on the same girl, huh?"

I laughed politely and counted the bills again, and counted the money in my wallet. "Hey, that's great," I said.

"You're in Rockefeller's class now?"

"Not quite, but at least I can pay my rent by the end of the week."

"Whattaya been doing?"

"Paying a day at a time. It's three-fifty a day, but the weekly rate is only twenty-one bucks, so I'll be getting one day a week free."

"Jesus. You're paying twenty-one bucks a week for a place to sleep?"

"That's right."

"Keed, that's *wrong*. Where you staying, the Ritz?"

"As a matter of fact it's a real dump. But at the price—"

"You're paying way too much, Chip."

"It's the cheapest hotel in Chicago. Or at least in the downtown area. I looked all over."

"Hotels!" He waved a great sigh and shook his head. "Hotels are for a night, two nights, a weekend maybe. Hotels aren't to live. Who the hell can afford it? Twenty-one bucks a week and you don't even get any meals or anything, is that right? Son of a bitch, you know what I pay? Eighty-five a month, and that's two rooms and a kitchen and a bathroom. You got a private bath in that hotel of yours?"

"No."

"I pay the same as you for Aileen and myself, an apartment instead of a room. That's what it costs you to live in that hotel of yours." He scratched his head. "Tell you the truth, I don't see how you can live. What did I pay you today, eleven dollars?"

"Ten and a half."

"Whatever it was. So three and a half from that for the room leaves seven, and figure a buck and a half each for breakfast and lunch is three from seven leaves four, and a decent dinner if you eat it out has to cost you two and a half bucks at the bottom, leaves you what? A dollar and a half? You can just about go to the movies." He shook his head again. "On top of which there's no work when it rains and no work when I got a big darkroom schedule. I don't know what I've paid you altogether over the past couple of weeks, but it can't come to all that much."

It didn't. I had worked six days out of the past nine, and my total earnings were $57.75. But then my expenses weren't as high as he had figured them. My breakfast was seventy cents and my dinner ranged from a dollar to a dollar-eighty. My lunch was generally a candy bar, and I had found a place where they only charged a nickel for a nickel bar. And sometimes I had a cup of coffee next door to the hotel before I went to sleep.

So actually I was saving money. I had hit Chicago two weeks before with $27.46 in my pocket, and I had earned $57.75 from Gregor and another twenty dollars and change on other jobs I had picked up a day at a time, and my current balance stood at just over $36.

At this rate, though, it was going to take me an awfully long time to become what you would call wealthy. Also I was due for some capital expenditures, if you want to call it that. Like washing my underwear and socks at night meant I had to put it on slightly damp in the mornings, which wasn't all that much fun. And it might be nice having another pair of pants and another shirt, not to mention the fact that the State Street sidewalks were having a bad effect on my shoes.

"Chip keed, I got an idea."

I looked at him.

"Suppose you could pay the same twenty-one bucks a week, or for the sake of convenience call it twenty, meaning you're saving a dollar right off the top, and you get a place to sleep and it's a clean place and all, and you share the bathroom with two people instead of three hundred, and on top of everything else, you get home-cooked breakfasts and dinners included. How's that sound?"

"Where is the place? Madrid?"

"Right here in beautiful Chicago. Just three blocks from here." One of the sunken eyes closed very slowly in what I had grown to recognize as a wink. "C'mon, keed, let's get our asses in gear. I gotta tell Aileen she's running a boardinghouse."

I was a little uncertain about this. I mean, it sounded great, and if anything it sounded too great. The only question was whether I wanted to get that tied up with Gregor. My job was doing menial labor for a failure, and that didn't quite fit in with my goal of a position with Opportunity For Advancement. Not that I figured Gregor would want to evict me if I went to work for somebody else. I was bright enough to realize that my room and board would just about pay the rent on his place, and I'm sure I wasn't the first of us to come to this realization. But I didn't know whether I wanted to be around him off the job as well as on it, and I didn't know if I wanted to be what amounted to a part of his family, sharing two rooms and a bath with him and Aileen.

Then I met Aileen.

* * *

I moved in that night. There wasn't all that much involved in moving in, since I didn't even have to go back to the hotel. The nice thing about not owning anything is that you don't have to go back for it. So when I say that I moved in, all it really amounts to is that I went to Gregor's apartment and met Aileen and had dinner and stayed the night.

It was a million miles away from the Eagle Hotel, believe me. Dinner was spaghetti and meatballs, and while it didn't fit the homemade label Gregor had hung on it—the spaghetti was out of a box and the sauce out of a can—it was still far better than the blue-plate special in a diner on Madison. And afterward we sat around in the living room and watched television and talked a little, and before they turned in Aileen made some more coffee (instant coffee) and brought out some A & P-brand jelly doughnuts, and afterward she gave me a sheet and a pillow and a pillowcase and they went to their room and left me the couch.

I wasted a lot of time and mental energy trying to figure out how to turn that couch into a bed. It wasn't designed to make the switch. It was just a couch, and by the time I figured this out for myself I was tired enough to sleep standing up in a closet.

I spread the sheet on the couch and got undressed and rolled up in the sheet. I wondered if I ought to buy a pair of pajamas or something. Then I wondered about Aileen, and if maybe she would come out and kiss me good-night or something.

She was pretty spectacular. Longish light blond hair and oval cat's eyes and high Slavic cheekbones and a full wet red mouth. She had the most goddamned suggestive mouth I have ever seen in my life. Her body reinforced the Lustful Peasant image in a big way. Large heavy pointed breasts, a hint of a belly, wide hips, large rounded bottom, big well-muscled thighs. The dress she wore was supposed to be a shapeless style. Only when she wore it, it took on a shape. It was really something amazing to watch her walk around in that thing, with all that flesh making interesting movements against the cloth of the dress.

I kept thinking about her, and imagining things. She was about the most sexual person I had ever met in my life. She just exuded this constant aura. It wasn't that she put out feelers or gave the impression that she was hot for me or anything, but even if she decked herself out in a nun's habit and cut her hair in a crew cut it would still be hard to spend ten seconds with her without imagining what she was like in bed.

I imagined she was fantastic. I imagined that she would make love like crazy, and that she would take a man and screw him absolutely blind (I now knew why Gregor's eyes seemed to be falling back into his head) and then, when she was done with you and you were deliciously half dead, she would wrap you up in her arms and legs and breasts and keep you warm as toast all through the night.

I kept on with this imagining, and you know how it is, what with one thing leading to another, well. There was a point when I realized that no one was going to break the mood by doing something creative with the plumbing, and I also realized that she was going to change my sheet in the morning, and maybe you can think of more embarrassing things to have happen, and maybe I can now, but I certainly couldn't then, and didn't even want to try.

The next afternoon I bought myself a second pair of socks.

"Now was I right or was I right?" Gregor said every now and then. "Here you're saving all kinds of money and living like a human being. Was I right?"

He was right, all right. Each morning I got up

bright and early and had a glass of unfrozen orange juice and a cup of instant coffee and a bowl of cornflakes or rice toasties or something like that. There was one of those undairy creamers to put on the cereal. The list of ingredients sounded like the secret formula for the hydrogen bomb, for Pete's sake. Well, there's nothing like home cooking.

Then, about five days out of eight, I would go to work for Gregor, putting in an average of six hours' work. When he had some developing and printing to do, I generally kept him company in the darkroom. He wanted to charge me for photography lessons. I got out of that one by offering to help him in the darkroom for a dollar an hour instead of a dollar and a half. We compromised; he didn't charge me, and he didn't pay me. It was fairly interesting, and I learned what the different chemicals were and what they did. I also learned that one place I didn't want to spend the rest of my life was in a darkroom.

On my days off, I sometimes picked up day work handing out passes for television shows or going door to door in some place like Oak Park, taking sample bars of a combination soap and cleansing cream (*Neither soap nor cleansing cream, but new improved Urglegurgleblech*) and rubberbanding them to people's doorknobs. It's against the law to put anything that's not mail into a mailbox, and they wouldn't fit under the door the way handbills do, so you had to loop them on the doorknob, which was very time consuming.

I took a few home for Aileen. You were expected to—what the hell, a sample was so people could sample it, no? But I didn't do what I really wanted to do, which was to stuff the whole batch of them down a sewer and go to the movies. For one thing, I had come to see that a man gets ahead in this world by doing his job to the best of his ability and playing fair with his employers. For another thing, a kid from Missouri dumped his soap and the crew chief caught him and beat the living shit out of him.

The rest of the time, when I wasn't working or helping in the darkroom, I divided between the apartment and the rest of Chicago. I would go out at night with no particular goal in mind, maybe stopping at the library for a while and then roaming around the city. The idea of meeting a girl of some sort or another was always in my mind, but then it always had been, and it had never done me any particular good before, and it didn't now, either. Most of the time, as a matter of fact, I never even saw a girl, or if I did she was with somebody.

There are supposed to be slightly more women than men in the country, but if you've ever wandered around a big city after dark you couldn't help becoming convinced that there are maybe twenty or thirty men on the open market for every woman. I don't know where the girls go at night, or what they do, but they aren't where the men are.

Once, in a sort of middle-class hippie place on Rush Street, I seemed to be doing pretty well with this girl with long hair and sunglasses. She was from some college. I told her I was a dropout, which wasn't all a lie. We were getting along fairly well, but then her date came back and that was the end of that. And another time a woman got interested in me at a diner. I was having coffee to keep warm and she was having coffee to sober up, I suppose, but it wasn't working. She had a puffy look, as if someone had taken a bicycle pump and put a little air in all the cells of her body. At first I thought she was about thirty-five, and the closer I looked the older she got. It was like watching the aging process through the modern miracle of time-lapse photography, as they say in the commercials.

We went and sat together in a booth in the back, and she kept breathing on me and dropping single entendres. She put her hand on my leg. Then she put her hand a little higher and gave me a friendly squeeze. By this time she looked about a hundred and eight and I got this all-embracing wave of nausea. I said I had to go to the toilet. I was half afraid she would follow me. I wouldn't really put it past her. I went to the john, and then I went to the back entrance and slipped out, leaving her to pay for my coffee and find some other boy to molest. I went out of my way to avoid that particular diner ever after.

And you know something, by the time I was a couple of blocks away from that woman, I called myself every name I could think of. I mean I really felt stupid. Obviously she was nothing spectacular, but the thing of it was that she was *there*, for Pete's sake, and she was *willing*. And it wasn't exactly as though I had to beat women off with a club. I was, let's face it, a very horny kid with a desperate desire to stop being a there's-that-dumb-word-again virgin. She could at least have served that purpose. I didn't have to love her to ball her. I didn't even have to like her.

That was as close as I came to scoring in the streets of Chicago, that and a couple of others and come-hither glances from faggots, with one of them going so far as to make a tentative grab for me while I was making use of an industrial bathroom fixture. I told them all no, and they all took no for an answer. I guess nobody found me exactly irresistible.

You might think, after all that, that I would have spent all my time around the apartment. I did spend a lot of it there, as a matter of fact, but what drove me out of there from time to time was the fact that Aileen was driving me right out of my mind.

It wasn't just what she looked like, which I told you about. It wasn't just that their bedroom door was not very substantial, and that I could hear them whenever they made love, which they did almost every night. (If they hadn't, I would have worried about Gregor. Really.) And it wasn't just that she was so sane and healthy about her physical self that she was completely casual about walking around half-naked in front of me, giving me groin-grabbing glimpses of one part of her after another until I literally ached.

It was that, on top of all of this, I was really digging her and Gregor as human beings. And it was a strange relationship, see, because I really didn't know what sort of relationship it was supposed to be. They were both a lot older than me. I think Gregor was in his forties, and I suppose she must have been close to thirty. So some of the time they were something like replacement parents, and since they had come into my life so shortly after my own parents left it, this did seem a logical role for them to play.

But I had never felt about my own mother as I felt constantly about Aileen. (Or if I did, I wasn't aware of it, and I'd just as soon not find out about it now, either, Dr. F.) If Aileen was my mother, then I was King Whatsisname with the broken ankles. And proud of it.

They were also like an older brother and older sister, and they were also like my boss and his wife, and they were also like my landlady and her husband, and, oh, it was too involved to keep straight. So the outcome was that I felt very comfortable and secure hanging around the apartment, reading a book or watching television or playing knock rummy with Gregor or helping Aileen with the dishes. I felt very comfortable almost all of the time, and then all at once, I would just have to get out of there before I started running around on all fours and chewing at the carpet.

I mean linoleum.

It was on a Friday night when Gregor got a phone call and said he had to go out. The first time this sort of thing had happened I got very ginchy about being left alone with Aileen, very hopeful and very anxious both at once, but nothing happened then, and after that I got accustomed to it and thought nothing of it. If anything, I found it very relaxing to be alone with her. I could talk to her when there were just the two of us in a way I couldn't with Gregor around. About my folks, for instance, and what I wanted out of life, and various heavy things it would have embarrassed me to talk about in front of Gregor. Aileen hardly ever said much, but she had a way of listening that went down very smoothly.

Gregor went out around eight-thirty, and Aileen and I talked and watched television for about an hour and a half. Then he came back looking happy.

"We're in business," he told her. "Mark can use as much as five hundred or a thou's worth of the right stuff." He turned to me. "A photography assignment, keed. You thought I made the whole nut snapping dummies in the street, didn't you? But sometimes something good comes up." To Aileen he said, "I've got the studio from now until four in the morning if I want it."

"You want to go there?"

"Right. And use the darkroom right there, and

deliver the goods in the morning. And have the money in my pocket before that kike changes his sonofabitching mind. You want to get ready, keed?"

"Me?"

"He means me," Aileen said.

"My prize model."

I said, "No kidding? You do the modeling?"

"That's how I found her, keed. My best and sweetest model. You ever look at the fashion magazines? *Vogue, Harper's Bazaar*—"

"Greg, put a sock in it, damn it."

He smiled at her. "Sure, they're all dying to give her a spread, aren't they, keed? And she'd give them a spread in return."

"Greg, in one minute you can go take pictures of soup cans."

"Just kidding."

"I mean with photographic artistry like yours, Greg, the subject's not really important, is it? You could go take artsy-craftsy shots of sewer gratings and the museums would stand in line for them."

"Baby, all I said—"

"I mean let's keep track of just who we all are, why don't we?"

This went on awhile. I had the feeling that I'd walked in on the last reel of a movie that only made sense if you'd seen the first part. I was still thinking it over while Gregor packed his gear and Aileen went off to change her clothes and make herself up. When they were ready, Greg started picking up his equipment, and I offered to help him carry it.

He said, "Well, sure, I suppose—" and she cut in to suggest that I come along and watch a photographic session.

"You futz around in the darkroom all the time, you might as well get acquainted with all sides of the photography business. Isn't that right, Greg?"

"You really think so?"

"Why not?"

"Well, it's fine with me, keed."

"It's certainly fine with me."

"If you say so."

"Because this would be a dumb time for modesty, I certainly think."

"If you say so."

"And Chip's practically one of the family, aren't you, honey?"

I listened to all of this without saying anything. I suppose you figured it out a long time ago, but then you're sitting down somewhere reading it all at once, while I was living it a little at a time. I knew there was a lot going on that I wasn't getting, but that was as far as I could go with it. I was lost, and waiting for someone to find me.

So we walked the couple of blocks to the office suite. It was empty except for a little guy at one of the desks who was catching up with his bookkeeping. He looked up when we came in and then looked down again. We ignored him and went into the studio. Gregor locked the door.

He set up his equipment and arranged various lights and things, explaining it all to me as he did it. I didn't catch much of what he was saying because I was too busy trying to figure out what I was missing.

Then he was ready, and Aileen gave an odd little smile and got up on top of this dark green velvet couch. She gave a tug and lifted her dress up over her head and tossed it across the room out of camera range.

There was nothing under it but Aileen.

Oh, I thought. Nude pictures. Cheesecake, so to speak. Now I understood.

But not entirely.

"It's a mutual thing we've got going." Aileen said, spreading her legs. "It's actually a beautiful relationship, Chip. See, Greg takes my picture, and in return I take his."

I looked at Greg. He was buried under the black cloth and looked as though he was part of the camera apparatus. I looked at Aileen again. She had her hands between her legs, one on each side of what I was looking at.

"Only I have a built-in camera," she was saying, "and I don't have to futz around with floodlights or exposure settings. I just take aim and snap away. Say cheese, Greg."

Greg didn't say anything. I suppose he was still under the hood.

I wasn't looking at him, actually.

My mouth was as dry as a sand sandwich and I had this weird chilly sweat all over my hands and feet and under my arms. And I couldn't quite catch my breath, and I couldn't stop shaking all over, and I couldn't take my eyes off the most fantastic thing I had ever seen in my life.

The shutter worked.

"Click!" Aileen said.

CHAPTER FOUR

FOR A LITTLE OVER AN HOUR I STOOD there with my eyes falling out of my head while Gregor took filthy pictures of his wife. After her opening round of flashy repartee, Aileen didn't have anything to say. Gregor stayed under the black cloth, and stayed quiet. And believe me, I didn't say word one. A lot of things came to mind, I'll admit, but I kept them to myself.

One idea that I couldn't get out of my head was that this was all a dream, and if that was so, I had to be very careful not to do anything to wake myself up before the dream turned wet. Because dream or no, I was in what you might term a state of advanced physical excitement.

It was really fantastic.

I don't know if I can clue you in as to just what it was like in that little room. (Which is probably a pretty dumb thing for me to say, for Pete's sake, because I'm supposed to be writing this, and if I can't handle it, that means I'm wasting both our time, and that it's going to be a long siege of Maine sardines and day-old bread.) Seriously, I could try to put down all the poses Aileen struck and to say which ones made me the horniest and all, and if I did this, well, you might begin to get your own idea of what it was like in there, but I'm not all that certain it would add up to anything.

Well, just as an idea of the whole approach the two of them had, this was how Gregor used up one particular roll of film. He did several rolls of individual series work, which came to an even dozen pictures, which would eventually get wrapped up and sold together, and which would tell some vague sort of a story.

This particular one was the banana series, and it started off with a muffled voice from under the black cloth saying, "The banana, keed." At which point Aileen got off the couch, went to Gregor's bag of tricks, found a pair of ripe bananas, and got back on the couch.

I remember seeing those pictures, the banana set, after they were developed and printed. And if you hit them in order and were in the frame of mind to believe them, it really looked as though old Aileen was getting her cookies that way. It was pretty realistic.

Only an hour or so had passed when Gregor came up for air. His forehead was dripping with sweat. I guess it was pretty hot under the black cloth. It wasn't all that cool anywhere else in the room, either.

"Wraps it up," he said. He dug his cigarettes out of his shirt pocket, lit one for himself, and offered the pack to me. I shook my head. Some people are just physically incapable of believing that some other people don't smoke. He tossed the pack and the matches to Aileen and she lit up and tossed them back. It was all very casual, almost athletic, with all of this underhand lobbing of cigarette packs and matchbooks. You could almost forget that Aileen was stark naked, and that she had spent the past hour holding her labia open and sucking on her own nipples and sticking bananas up herself. (I don't know if I ought to be quite that graphic about it, but that was what she was doing, and I think it would be worse to try being coy about it, for Pete's sake. I mean, if you're going to come right out and say that a woman posed for a batch of dirty pictures while you stood there watching, you might as well call a spade a spade, right?)

Aileen blew out a cloud of smoke. She said, "Is that all you want to shoot?"

"I think so, yeah."

"I thought you were going to take some pornographic ones."

I didn't do an enormous double take on that line. I just thought I was hearing wrong.

But he said, "Hard-core? No, the sonofabitching timer is on the fritz. I don't know what's the matter with it. Less than two years old and it just went. Nothing works anymore and nobody gives a damn. The whole civilization is coming apart at the seams."

I must have looked puzzled. Aileen said, "It's a timer on the shutter. He sets up the shot and then he has fifteen seconds to get in the picture with me."

"Twelve seconds," Gregor said.

She ignored the correction. "That way we can do the more interesting things, Chip. What you could call hard-core pornography."

I nodded.

"What we shot now tonight is called soft-core."

"What's the difference?"

"Redeeming social importance," Gregor said.

"Huh?"

"That's what the Supreme Court calls it. You know, that you can argue it's a work of art and not a hundred percent obscene. If you actually show people fucking, then it's considered a hundred percent obscene."

"In hard-core pornography," Aileen said, "the man's core is hard."

"That's an old gag," Gregor said.

"Professional humor," she said.

"But the point is that the timer is on the bum." He sucked on his cigarette and clucked his tongue pensively. "I'll tell you something, you wouldn't believe what a short time twelve seconds is until you tried to set up a shot and then get in it yourself. You know the worst part?"

"What?" I managed to ask.

"Staying up. You know, erect." His eyes dropped to his trouser front, and mine fought the impulse to follow. "When you set up with the camera and all, you know, your whole concentration is on technical matters. You don't even think sex. You might have trouble believing this, but when I'm taking these pictures, there's no difference in my mind whether I'm taking a picture of Aileen playing with herself or of the Chicago skyline. It's all the same as far as I'm concerned."

He was right. I had trouble believing this. I had seen the Chicago skyline, and I had seen Aileen playing with herself, and there was no chance I would ever get the two of them mixed up in my mind.

"So I set up a shot," he went on, "and then I have to turn on the excitement so that I'll get erect, and then rush rush rush to get into the right position before the sonofabitching shutter goes bang. It's the most nerve-racking thing going. And the thing is, the way I like to work, you know, is to shoot as much film as fast as I can, just one picture after the other. Just keep watching through the viewer and click them off whenever the pose is right. And the same way, Aileen likes to get into the spirit of a sequence and let it build the right way."

"To a climax," she said, with a wink.

"Yeah, to a climax," he said winklessly. "It's the same as whatchamacallit, method acting. Living the part. Look, you don't know the business, but I can tell you that if you looked at a set of the keed's photos and a set of the average model, there would be all the difference in the world." I had no trouble believing this. "The average girl, she'll put on this sonofabitching mechanical smile that looks painted on her face, or maybe she'll pout a little, and there's nothing the least bit natural about it. Aileen, she's something else. Sometimes I think she has, you know, a climax. Just going through the poses."

"Sometimes," she said, "she does."

"But without the timer," he said, and then he dropped his jaw a few inches and actually snapped his fingers. "Hey," he said, as an imaginary lightbulb formed over his head. "Now why the hell didn't I think of that before?"

"Of what?"

He pointed at me. "You," he said. "You could take the pictures. You want to be a photographer, you got to start sooner or later."

While I was busy not saying anything, Aileen said, "I've got a better idea. Chip's a smart kid, but he doesn't know anything about photography. You can't expect him to have your touch with a camera."

"Well, that's true," Gregor said.

"And anyway, I think the world's getting tired of the same old pictures of you and me, honey. But suppose you take the pictures and Chip and I star in them?"

They had done this before, Aileen assured me. Twice, as a matter of fact, with a fellow who neither of them really knew very well, as another matter of fact. And it was really perfectly legitimate as far as she was concerned, because after all it wasn't really sexual. Which was to say that they really didn't do anything. They would just set up a shot and Gregor would shoot it and then they would swing into another position.

The other fellow never actually got inside of her, Gregor explained. And that, he said, was an absolute requirement as far as he was concerned. Because while he and Aileen might have a more liberal attitude in certain respects than the average married couple, in other respects they were what you might call old-fashioned, and one of the respects in which they were old-fashioned was that neither of them believed in having sex outside of marriage. He was absolutely faithful to Aileen, and she in turn was a hundred percent faithful to him, and that was the way it had to be.

The two of them took turns explaining these things and filling me in on the fine points of pornographic photography, and let me tell you, it was the weirdest conversation ever. I wasn't tonguetied all the way through it, but I think I might as well have been. I would ask various dumb questions and they would chime in with the answers. Wouldn't Gregor be upset just seeing me in these various poses with Aileen?

"No, keed, because I know it doesn't mean anything and nothing's really happening."

Wouldn't Aileen be embarrassed by doing that sort of thing in front of her husband?

"Embarrassed, Chip? I've got a huge streak of exhibitionism in me. You must have figured that out for yourself. If anything, I got a kind of a kick out of you watching just now, during the soft-core shots. And you know, honey, I like you, and Greg likes you, and if anything I think it would be kind of, you know, fun."

Fun.

"We got time," Gregor said. "We got all night here and in one of the darkrooms, and we can probably use both darkrooms if it comes to that because I don't think the other one is booked at this hour. There would be a lot more dough if I had hard stuff for Mark. If you wanted to do it, well, I suppose I could pay you, and I don't mean any of that buck-and-a-half-an-hour crap. I could afford, oh, what the hell, let's say twenty bucks."

"Greg, honey, how on earth can you be so damn cheap?" She turned to me and grinned conspiratorially. "He'll pay you fifty dollars, Chip. How does that sound?"

After a few seconds passed, I realized we were all waiting for me to come up with an answer. "It sounds fine," I squeaked. If my voice had been any higher they would have thought I wasn't old enough for the job.

"Well, that's fine," Gregor said. "Fifty dollars—well, sure, I suppose so. The only question, and I guess nobody but you knows the answer, keed, if you know it yourself, is whether or not you'll be able to perform. Most of the time you can fake it, you know, but some of the shots have to show you—"

"With a hard core," Aileen put in. She rolled her eyes in exasperation. "Gawd," she said. "Of all the stupid questions to ask him. He's had the hardest core in America for the past hour and a half, haven't you, honey? So I don't think he's going to have troubles now."

We got things off to a sensational start by having Aileen put on her dress and shoes. And oddly enough the sight of her with clothes on really got to me. I'm not being sarcastic. I had just about gotten to the point where I was used to her being naked, and now that she had the dress on again I was taking it back off again mentally and remembering what she looked like without it and getting hornier than ever at the memory.

She sat down and patted the couch next to her,

and I sat, and she looked at me and gave me a grin as big as O'Hare Airport. I don't know if I can explain it, but when she grinned that way I knew that things were going to be all right, that this was my mother-sister-friend-landlady-sweetheart Aileen, and that we were going to have a little innocent fun together without anybody getting messed up. You may have trouble figuring out how she packed all that into a three-second grin, but it was all there and I read it loud and clear.

"Now the whole thing is to get into the part," she said. "You tell yourself that you and I are crazy about each other and that I'm very desirable and we're alone together and we're going to make love. Don't even think about the camera for now. It's just a little clicking noise; it's nothing to think about. And don't worry about striking poses, or what angles Greg's shooting from. Just get into the spirit of the thing and we'll wind up with some decent shots."

I thought, *Decent?* And then she puckered up invitingly, and I leaned forward, not too sure what came first, and we actually kissed.

That's an understatement. We went right off the bat into a deep soul kiss, and not because it was my idea. I was too dumb to think of it, but before

I could think of anything at all, her tongue was halfway down my throat and her breasts were pressing against me.

Click!

We held the kiss, and she shifted a little and took my hand and put it on the front of her dress, over her breast. I gave a gentle squeeze and felt the nipple stiffen.

Click!

She wriggled her hips invitingly. I put my hand under her dress and touched the inside of her thigh. She felt like—I was going to say silk, but it was more like warm glass, except even smoother somehow. I felt the play of muscles in her leg. Her kissing got greedier. She was sucking on my tongue as if she wanted to swallow it.

Click!

If this was method acting, I know why they use it. Maybe she liked to think we were just going through the motions, and maybe Gregor liked to think it, but if they really believed it they were both fruity as a nutcake because Aileen was hot enough to burn. I let my hand move higher, and my mind filled up with what I had seen earlier, those pink thighs and that puff of curly blond hair and all, and I touched her and she was all warm and wet, and—

Click!
Jesus Christ.
Click!

I let her take the lead. It seemed only natural, since she was the experienced one in every sense. Besides, I never wanted to move out of one pose in order to get into another. But she gave a reluctant sigh and steered us to the next bend in the river, which consisted of her opening the dress to the waist and letting me amuse myself with her breasts.

Click!
By handling them.
Click!
And kissing them.
Click!
And so on.
Click!

I'm putting all the clicks in to give you an idea of what Gregor was doing, but don't get the impression that I was always aware of the camera. Some of the time it was as though it wasn't there at all and the whole sex thing between me and Aileen was entirely real. Then that sensation would fade, and I would be so completely aware of the camera that I almost couldn't stand it. Then the clicks would seem loud enough to break glass, and I would start feeling like a machine making love to another machine. But this never lasted long enough to let me cool down, and each time I got into the mood completely again I would just be that much hotter than I was before.

It didn't take long for both of us to get out of our clothes. Aileen had already been giving my groin some gentle feels now and then, so exposing myself was no big deal to me, and as for Gregor, I wasn't very keenly aware of him just then.

Click!

I did have a second or so of concern after I got out of my shorts when I saw that she was looking at me. I guess every man who ever lived must have done a certain amount of worrying about his equipment at one time or another. And while I don't think I was more hung up on the subject that most, there were times when I wondered whether it was too small, or funny looking, or ugly, or I don't know what. Since I had no way of knowing how you could tell a pretty one from an ugly one, or how much was enough, there was no real way to avoid these worries completely.

So I had that flash of anxiety. But the next second Aileen's eyes went from the area in question to my eyes, and she gave that grin again, the same as before, and her lips parted just wide enough to admit her tongue, and she ran her tongue hungrily around her lips, and got the most beautifully lustful look in her eyes—

Click!

I hadn't felt so proud since I got my first quarter from the tooth fairy.

She touched me a little, and I'm sure the shutter went on clicking, but I didn't hear it. Then she got up on the couch and stretched out on her back with her knees bent. She motioned me on top, and we touched bodies from chest to groin, and my thing proved it had a mind of its own by going straight for her thing. I no sooner touched her than she gave a quick twitch of her hips and got out of the way.

"Easy," she murmured. "Remember the rules, Chip. The sign on the door says *Private*, remember? *Admission Restricted To Authorized Personnel.*"

I wanted to cry with disappointment. I had begun to think, somewhere along the line, that all of that business about not going all the way had been, well, something we would conveniently forget when the time came. I had put it in the same bag with her statement that none of this was really sexual.

I thought about just going ahead and doing it. I could always pretend it was an accident, I thought. Just put it where it belonged and keep it there long enough to finish, and even if she thought it was rape, she wouldn't be likely to go running through the streets shouting for a cop. And if she and Gregor got mad, well, the hell with them. Whatever happened, I would at least have done the one thing on earth I really wanted to do.

Lots of luck. I gave a well-intentioned thrust, and the shutter clicked behind me, and Aileen got out of the way with no trouble at all.

"Naughty," she whispered. *"Bad boy."*

I guess I could never make it as a rapist.

At this point it really did become pretty artificial and mechanical and phony. We stopped pretending and just went through the motions as quickly and effortlessly as possible, and it made for a lot less nervousness for both of us (and maybe for all three of us, because I don't think Gregor was happy seeing his faithful wife an inch away from technical infidelity). So what we did was just get quickly into a position, take shots of it from two different angles, and then get into another position. I had done a lot of extracurricular reading over the years—I suppose that's pretty obvious, for Pete's sake—but even with all the times I went through the *Kama Sutra* and the *Ananga*

Ranga and *Eros and Capricorn* and *The Perverted Village* I had never quite realized how many different positions there are to not quite have sexual intercourse in.

Click!

Click!

Clickety clickety click!

By the time Gregor suggested we all stop for a cigarette break, I had reached a stage where I was just as glad to relax for a while. Not that I was relaxed in any meaningful sense of the word. I mean, face it, this wasn't a relaxing way to spend the evening. It just plain wasn't.

"Got some great shots," he said through a cloud of blue-gray smoke. "You want to know something, keed, you're a natural born actor. And how about the wife, huh? One great little actress."

He turned the key in the lock, peeked out. "Nobody home," he said. "Hang on a minute."

While he was gone I whispered to Aileen that I was going out of my mind.

"Poor baby," she said.

"I mean I don't think I can walk."

"You forgot the rules for a minute there, Chip. I've never done it with anyone but Greg. Not since I met him, and it's been almost six years now. You have to understand."

"I suppose so."

"You know, you're very nice-looking."

"Oh, come off it."

"You mean you don't know it yourself? You're a good-looking guy, and you've got a dreamy body."

"Cut it out. My bones stick out, for Pete's sake."

"I like the way you look."

"I mean—"

"I think we'll look good together."

She was beginning to get to me all over again. I started to say something, God knows what, but then Gregor came back in with his bottle of shitty peach-flavored brandy. I had the most unbelievable urge to take the bottle and shove it up his ass. I had the feeling that if I could just get him out of the picture, him and his goddamned camera, I could spend the rest of my life balling Aileen, and I couldn't think of any way I'd rather spend it.

He was saying that he thought we were all entitled to a drink. He tended to think of alcohol as a reward. I didn't know if I could hack the taste of that crud just then.

Aileen said, "Honey, I think just a short one, unless you're out of film."

"There's plenty," he said. "Why?"

"I thought like one more roll, that's all. I didn't do anything oral."

"I didn't know you were going to do that," he said warily. "I didn't even think of it."

"Well, it would be a case of faking it, really."

"I suppose," he said. "Son of a bitch, if they don't go for that stuff. You sure you want to?"

"Oh, I don't mind."

I went over and sat on the couch while he took a quick pull on the brandy bottle and then disappeared beneath the black cloth and went to work loading the camera with a fresh roll. Aileen finished her cigarette and came over and sat down next to me.

I reached for her.

"Not just yet," Gregor called out cheerfully. "I'll be set in a sec, keed."

"Aileen," I whispered, "you'll drive me up the walls."

"Poor baby."

"Look, I—"

She ran her tongue over her lips. This was a little trick of hers that didn't exactly leave me cold when she did it first thing in the morning over instant coffee and cold cornflakes. Now it was absolutely criminal.

"You'll like this," she said.

"Ready to roll," Gregor said.

"God in Heaven," I said.

"Lie down, baby." Her mouth was inches from my ear, blowing into it as she whispered. "Poor baby has had a mean night, huh? Mama will fix." Her hand moved over my chest and belly. My stomach contracted violently. "Ticklish," she murmured, blowing into my ear some more. The hand went on its merry way and grabbed. "Got small again," she said. "But Mama's gonna fix that, too."

Click!

I really felt like a baby, too. I lay there like a lump and felt so small and weak and helpless and so goddamned young I wanted to curl up and die. She kissed me on the mouth, and then on the throat, and then her mouth moved downward so that her long blond hair brushed over my face and chest and stomach.

Click!

I had my eyes closed, and my body was sort of stretched out the way you do when you float on your back in a swimming pool. I had that same kind of buoyant feeling, too.

She kissed it, and her hands did things, and the camera made stupid clicking noises, and the hard core was harder than ever. I could feel the blood in my head and I thought I was going to have a brain hemorrhage and die.

She did a million teasing things with her mouth. But there wasn't any contact to speak of.

Just her warm breath.

Click!

Breathing in and out, in and out.

Moistly.

Oh God, I thought, oh God, don't stop, for Christ's sake don't stop, whatever you do, don't stop, just another minute, just another second, God, don't stop—

Click!

And she stopped.

Since then I must have tried a thousand times to figure out why she bothered getting started if she wasn't going to finish it. I mean, face it, it's not as though she was some drippy virgin who didn't realize that a man had to finish what he started or get horribly frustrated. Everybody knows this; anybody old enough to read Ann Landers' column can figure it out. And Aileen was a long ways from a virgin. She may not have slept with anybody but Gregor since they were married, but I'm sure she must have had a few hundred men before he came around.

So she obviously knew what she was doing, but then why do it? She wasn't a cruel person. She was nice, really, and she seemed to like me.

I mean, I could understand why she felt compelled to perform the act without any actual contact. That is, I could understand it about as well as I could understand why it was all right for us to pet like crazy but not all right for me to get into her. Which is to say that I didn't understand and it didn't make any sense but at least I knew the basic rules of the game.

But if she was going to leave me high and dry, why start anything in the first place? What was the point? Gregor had been ready to pack up and go. So had I. And she hadn't wanted to have anything done to her. I was just supposed to lie there and leave everything to her, and I did, and it hadn't ended quite the way I had hoped.

I lay there like an overwound watch, going pingpingping inside and staying drawn hellishly tight. I couldn't talk or think or breathe or see. I didn't know where she was, but I knew where she belonged. In Hell, with a hot poker rammed up her behind.

And then I heard her voice, talking, not to me, but beyond me, to Gregor:

"Honey, baby, I have to give him some relief. He's a kid, you know, and I guess it was all too much for him. The excitement. Being with me, and in front of the camera and all, and going through the motions, and the different positions, and then this last thing. I think it stopped being just an act for him, and he got very excited, and if you look at him now, you can see how tense he is."

"So?"

"I have to do something."

"Well, I don't—"

"I wouldn't be unfaithful."

"Because I wouldn't like that, keed."

"And I wouldn't do it."

"I should hope not. I should just sonofabitching hope you wouldn't."

Her hand on my leg.

"But this would be just like a massage. I knew a girl who was a nurse in a hospital—"

"That's the best place to be a nurse."

"—and she told me how they used to give the patients rubdowns all the time, and if they got excited they would give that a rubdown, too, and that isn't wrong, do you think?"

"I suppose not."

Her hand gripped me.

"Of course it isn't," she said, her voice softer than ever now, and now she was talking less to him than to me, and her words moved in a jerky rhythm as her soft sure hand moved up and down, up and down, pumping up and down.

"Of course ... it isn't ... wrong ... baby ... baby ... it's all right ... all right ..."

Not like this, I thought. Not with your hand, and not in the middle of the air, not like this.

"It's all *right* ... it's all *right* ... it's all *right* ... it's all *right* ..."

Oh, yeah, I thought. Okay. Sure, sure, oh.

"It's all *RIGHT!*"

It was all right, all right.

CHAPTER FIVE

THE NEXT DAY GREGOR DIDN'T BOTHER doing his sidewalk photographer number. He went off to see Mark Somebody to turn a suitcase full of dirty pictures into as much money as possible.

"Soon as I get back, keed," he said, "you get your twenty-five smackers."

"Fifty," I reminded him.

"Oh, sure. My mistake."

"Sure."

As soon as he was out the door, I went into the kitchen and cornered Aileen. She asked me how come I wasn't working that morning. I said that a photographer's assistant didn't have much to do when the photographer wasn't on the job. There wasn't much point in me handing out the little yellow cards if there was nobody on hand to take the pictures.

"I meant one of your other jobs," she said.

"Well, I didn't think I'd bother today. I earned fifty bucks last night."

"You make sure Greg gives you the whole fifty, Chip. Sometimes he tries to chisel people."

"He already tried."

"Well, you get the whole fifty. You worked for it."

"Yeah."

I wanted to reach for her but I didn't quite know how to go about it. You can't imagine how god-damned awkward the whole thing was. I mean, here we had gotten in this wild tangle the night before, with results that I told you about in probably too much detail already, so we won't go into that all over again, and now here it was morning and she was in the kitchen, wearing an apron and rinsing out coffee cups, and her whole attitude left me feeling that last night had never happened, that it was another dream of mine and when I woke up I would have a damp sticky sock in the bed with me. I mean, I knew it wasn't a dream, but it might as well have been.

"Chip?"

"What?"

"Are you angry with me?"

I looked at her. "Why should I be?"

"Because I teased you last night."

"Well, I knew what I was getting into."

"What you weren't getting into, you mean."

"Well."

"You're not angry?"

"No."

"I'm glad." She grinned quickly. "Because I like you a lot, Chip."

This time I did reach for her, and she moved her head aside, and I missed. I suppose practically any woman can make practically any man feel like an idiot, but it seemed to me that either she was particularly good at it or that I was particularly inept.

She said, "Last night was business, Chip."

"Yeah, sure."

"I'm not going to say I didn't enjoy it."

"You enjoyed it, huh?"

"Why, of course I did. I don't think there's anything wrong with enjoying your work, do you?"

"I guess not."

"I should certainly hope not." She put the dish towel on the drainboard and walked past me to the living room. There wasn't an abundance of room in the kitchen, and she managed to brush against me pretty good on the way, giving me the full treatment with that round rear end of hers. She got to me, all right. I suppose I'm pretty easy to get to, generally speaking, but old Aileen had a real knack for it as far as I was concerned.

I followed her into the living room. She went around straightening things up and emptying ashtrays, talking as she went. "There's nothing wrong with enjoying any kind of work," she went on. "I wouldn't pose for those pictures if I didn't get a certain amount of kick out of it. I like to think of all those people looking at pictures of me and getting excited. Sometimes I stop and think that there are men all over the country looking at naked pictures of me and playing with themselves. Having sex with me in their minds. And couples looking at different pictures of me, either alone or with someone, and getting so hot and bothered that they want to make love. When I think about that sort of thing I get a very strange feeling."

"Sure," I said.

She put an ashtray back on a tabletop and turned to look at me. "Just think of all the people who will look at those pictures of the two of us," she said.

"Yeah."

"Do you like the idea?"

"I don't know. I got bothered by that before. I mean, I thought somebody might recognize me, but then I thought that I didn't have anybody to care one way or the other. If some jerk I went to some school with saw it, well, what do I care? You know, let him envy me, let him eat his heart out. If I had any family it might be different, I guess."

"Poor baby. All alone in the world."

"Don't call me that."

"I called you that last night."

"I know."

She crossed to the television set, switched it on, collapsed neatly on the couch. My couch. She patted the cushion next to her, and I remembered how she had given the same invitational pat to the green couch in the studio last night. I felt lightheaded and shaky.

I pretended not to notice the invitation. "I think I'll have another cup of coffee," I told her. "You want one?"

"I'll make them."

"No, stay there," I said. "I, uh, I need the exercise."

She was still sitting in the same spot when I brought back the two cups of coffee. She said, "You know, Chip, that was fun last night."

"Here's your coffee."

"For you, too." She put the cup down next to mine on the coffee table. "We could have a lot of fun, you know. There are lots of times like this morning when Gregor is out and I'm home all alone. If you didn't try to force things, we could have a real good time."

"What kind of a real good time?"

"Like last night. Except without anybody watching or snapping pictures."

"And without finishing what we started."

She raised her eyebrows. "You finished, didn't you? I spent half an hour wiping the floor. If that wasn't what you would call finishing—"

"You know what I mean."

She put her hand on my cheek. "Didn't you get your kicks last night, baby?"

"I wanted to do it the right way."

"There's no right way, honey. Sex may be a game but there's no yo-yo keeping score. Whatever turns you on, that's the right way."

"I never got laid in my life, Aileen."

I turned away as I said this. I felt excited and happy and miserable all at the same time, and all tied in knots. She had my hand in both of hers and was petting it.

"I know that, Chip."

"It's pretty obvious, huh?"

"Well, reading between the lines of what you said. It's a big thing for you, huh? Being all hung up about being a virgin."

I nodded.

"Being a virgin, you know, it's something everybody is and something everybody gets over sooner or later. Even I was a virgin once. You may find that hard to believe—"

"Cut it out, will you?"

"Hey." I turned and looked at her. She gave me the wise grin, and some of the tension went out of me. "Now listen a minute, baby," she said. "We can have a little fun, if you want, or we can just let it stay nice and loose between us, if you'd rather have it that way, but one thing not to do is be so serious about everything, because that's nothing but a big bringdown."

I nodded again. "But why can't we—"

"Because we can't. Because that's where I draw the line. That's for Greg and nobody else. Look, if all you want to do is stick it in, you can go out and find a pro. You're getting fifty dollars from Greg. You're a rich man. If you want to just get on top of some syphilitic pig and get rid of your precious cherry, all you have to do—"

"You know what I want."

"Uh-huh, baby, but I also know what *I* want. And that's some nice tender sweetness from my baby, and you don't have to worry, I won't tease, I won't leave you frustrated. You'll come, honey, and so will I, and it'll be very nice, just leave everything to me."

"I don't know what to say."

"What's to say?" She laughed deep in her throat. "Come here," she said. "Do something brilliant, like kissing me."

Do you have any idea how many ways there are to do it without really doing it?

Neither did I.

There's just no end to the possibilities. There were just three rules to the game—or one rule, actually, that closed three doors to me. What it boiled down to, really, was that I couldn't enter her. (With what she still liked to call my hard core, that is. Other things, yes.) I guess there's precedent for this. In the legal definitions of rape and sodomy and other nice things like that, the dividing line is that same line Aileen used. Penetration. If you don't get in, the argument goes, then you haven't really Done Anything Wrong.

We didn't Do Anything Wrong.

But we did just about everything else.

You know something? I've thought about it, and I've come to the conclusion that if only I hadn't been a virgin at the time, I would have been the happiest man on earth. Because from a physical standpoint there was nothing frustrating about the relationship we had. I was getting there, and not in the therapeutic massage way I had made it in the photo studio, either. We weren't playing that little game at all. It had been strictly for Gregor's benefit, and now that we were on our own, we didn't try to hide the fact that the name of the game was Getting Kicks.

Sometimes we spent five or six hours in a row on that couch, and by the time we stopped I had made it so many times that I didn't have the strength to lift a finger, let alone my unhard core. So in simple terms of the amount of sex I was getting I was in the class of a man on a honeymoon with a nymphomaniac, for Pete's sake.

So in that sense it was really great. The more I got the more I wanted, and the more I wanted the more I got, and it looked as though it could just go on that way forever and it would keep getting better all the time.

Here's a comparison that you might want to pass up if you're very heavy on religion. Not to offend anybody, but I think it fits. It was like being

Adam and Eve in the Garden of Eden, with Paradise there, just everything you could want all spread out for you, except for these two trees that you couldn't go near. You could eat anything else in the world but the fruit of the Tree of Life and the Tree of Knowledge, so naturally what did you want? Right the first time. Well, so did I. The fruit was a cherry instead of an apple, and I wanted to get rid of it, not take a bite out of it, but otherwise it added up to about the same thing.

(Incidentally, suppose Adam and Eve ate from the Tree of Life instead of the Tree of Knowledge. Or from both of them. They'd still be alive, and the earth would be up to its neck in people. That doesn't have anything to do with anything else, but it's been bothering me ever since I was a little kid so I thought I would put it in. I'm supposed to be writing this straightforward, keeping to the subject and everything, but I was also told that the book ought to let the reader know how I feel about things and the kind of person I am, and frankly I think if I have to just tell everything absolutely cold and straight without putting down other things that come into my head while I'm sitting here, then the book might as well have been written by a machine. When I read a book, I like to have the feeling that a real human being actually sat down and wrote it, and that reading it will let me know something about him. Some books give you the feeling that the sheets of paper came out of the paper mill with the words already on them, for Pete's sake. Untouched by human hands, like the plastic food in turnpike restaurants.)

Well, to get back to what I was saying, if you're still with me, I sort of wish I could have rearranged my schedule so that I could have met Aileen five years later in life. That would have been perfect, I think. By then I would be twenty-two and years past being a virgin, but still young enough so that she would be the older woman showing me new ways to be the happiest kid on the block.

As it was, maybe I should have gone out and spent my fifty dollars (Gregor paid off in full, although he did make a halfhearted effort to make me settle for forty) on some professional prostitute. If I just could have crossed that barrier I would have stopped brooding about it. Or maybe I wouldn't. I guess not, really. I guess it would be impossible for anyone in his right or wrong mind not to want to ball that woman in every way there was.

I got to Chicago in late February, I was at the Eagle Hotel for about two weeks, I moved in with

Gregor and Aileen about three weeks before we had the picture-taking session, and it was Memorial Day weekend when I got out of there. I just worked it all out with paper and pencil to save you the trouble, assuming you're interested, and the way I figure it there was a stretch of about six weeks between the night we took the pictures and the morning I left Chicago.

When I think back on it, sometimes it seems as though it couldn't possibly have been that long, and other times it seems as though it must have been closer to six months. They were six fantastic weeks no matter how you look at it. In all that time we never once crossed any of the cruddy lines she had drawn, and Gregor never got any idea of what was going on, and I don't think we once went as much as thirty hours in a row without having a shot at it. It wasn't always a five-hour stretch on the couch (although that happened plenty of the time) and sometimes it was just a fast fingering at the kitchen sink or a quick hand job at the breakfast table. But it was as steady as a pension from the Federal Government.

I remember one night when she slipped out of the bedroom after Gregor had zonked out. She did this quite a few times, and since she and Gregor generally knocked one off before going to sleep, the goods I was getting weren't exactly untouched by human hands. Sloppy seconds, I think they call it. (Not really sloppy, because she would wash up first, but even so it used to bother me. At first, that is. You might be amazed the way a person can get used to things, and can stop being bothered by things that used to bother him.)

This one particular night a couple of winks and hand signals during the late movie had given me the message that I could expect company. So I was waiting for her from the minute she and Gregor closed their bedroom door, and the sound of their bedsprings was background music while I thought of all the things I wanted to do to Aileen. I was developing a pretty wicked imagination along those lines.

Then the door finally opened, and she tiptoed across to the bathroom, and I heard water running. And then she tiptoed some more, from the bathroom across the floor to the couch.

I pretended to be sleeping. We both knew it was a pretty transparent act, but she liked to find ways to wake me up. She kept finding ways, and they always worked. I'll bet she could do the Indian rope trick just by touching the rope with those hands of hers.

Well, not to go off on tangents, I woke up, and

she got on the couch with me, and we did things. Between her thighs, or under her arm, or in her hands, or between her breasts, or in the cleft of her buttocks, or—well, you name it. We made it, and I stretched out, and she curled up in my arms, and I felt like the King of the World.

"Oh, baby," she said. "You're so good for me."

I said, "Purr." Or something along those lines.

"You know what? I feel like a girl."

"You sure do."

"I'm serious."

I ran a hand over her. "You feel like a girl, all right. I'm glad, too, you know. I don't think I'd get as much of a kick out of all of this if you felt like a boy. I like these, see, and this, and—"

And a little later, when we came up for a breath of fresh air:

"Hey, I meant it before, clown. You make me feel like a girl again."

"You're not so old."

"Thanks a bunch."

"You're not that much older than I am, for Pete's sake. You do this mother bit all the time, but you're not exactly in the category of an antique."

"Keep saying it, baby."

"How old are you, anyway?"

"A hundred and ten."

"Shit."

"You know why you make me feel so young? Hey, that's a song. No, it's because of what we do. Necking and petting and fooling around like a couple of kids. It takes me back to when I was, you know, younger. And a virgin."

"I didn't know you ever were."

"Don't be a sharp-tongued son of a bitch, Chip. Your boyish charm is your biggest asset. Don't piss it away."

"I'll bear that in mind."

"Please do." She put her hand between my legs and gave me a reassuring pat. "Yeah, I was a virgin once upon a time. Isn't that remarkable? And when I'm with you I'm a virgin all over again, and the whole sex business is, I don't know, cleaner and hungrier and hornier and everything rolled into one. It takes me back, it really does."

"Being in bed with me."

"Uh-huh."

"Sort of like hearing an old song on the radio that was popular when you were a kid. An oldie but goodie."

I couldn't see her face in the dark, but I guess she raised her eyebrows at that one. She had that tone in her voice, saying, "You making fun of me, Chip?"

"No."

"I think you were, at least a little, maybe. Yeah, like hearing an old song, in a kind of way. The way a song or anything like that makes you feel the way you used to. Sometimes I'll walk outside during the late summer when there's a wet wind blowing off the lake, on like a really warm lazy night, and I'll walk around the block or something and the air will be the way it is in Florida. Just the right temperature and humidity, I suppose. What's the word? Sultry? But before this can even go through my mind, I'll get this feeling of being seventeen years old again, because I spent a summer in Florida when I was seventeen."

"You were in Florida? I thought you were always in Chicago."

"Oh, I would travel from time to time."

"What were you doing in Florida?"

"Fucking."

"That was a straight question."

"Well, it was a straight answer, honey bunch."

"At seventeen? I guess I'm retarded."

"Worry about it, why don't you?"

"I do, I do. When did you start?"

"Huh?"

"When did you start making love?"

"What are you, Mr. District Attorney? I never

started. I'm a virgin, baby doll. Handle me with care." And, huskily, "If we keep on talking we'll wake Greg, and he might take a dim view of this. So let's not talk anymore. Why don't I just lie here and you can lick different parts of me and see whether or not I like it? Sort of what you might call a scientific experiment."

(I was just thinking, looking at the last part, that I'll bet it's word for word the way that conversation actually went. Obviously, since I'm putting all of this on paper after it happened, I'm just getting the dialogue as close as possible to the way it happened. I didn't wander through life with a tape recorder hanging around my neck, and I'm not the total recall type. I'm not absolutely convinced *anybody* is, and there are times when I think people who pretend to be are full of crap. But this one conversation stuck in my mind very vividly. I can hear her speaking the words even now, as if I were playing myself a record of the conversation.

(I guess that's because I thought about it so many times since then. And it struck me, and strikes me now, that it was a strange combination of games that Aileen was playing. First there was the bit about feeling like a girl, a virgin. And at the same time she kept coming on with the older-but-wiser routine and a heavy dose of the mother image. I couldn't understand how she could be a virgin and a mother at the same time. As far as I know, that only happened once.)

During the six weeks of trading orgasms with Aileen, her genius of a husband never suspected a thing. I'm just about a hundred percent certain of that. I went on working with him, and I saw him at meals and during the evening, and neither of us acted any differently toward one another than we did before. I had thought for a while that I would be eaten up with guilt over what I was doing with Aileen. No such thing. It may be that I'm just not the type for guilt, that I'm of such low moral character that I can live under a man's roof and take his money and share his bread and not feel bad about taking his beloved wife to bed. I think, though, that there's more to it than that.

After all, I wasn't doing a thing to Aileen behind his back that I hadn't done to her right in front of him, with his approval. (Well, that's pushing it, I guess; we did enlarge our bag of tricks, after all, and we went at them with a hell of a lot more enthusiasm. But you get the idea.) And she was still being faithful to him as far as their joint idea of fidelity was concerned. And, more than anything else, I knew damned well that I wasn't taking anything away from Gregor. Just by listening to the creak of his bedsprings I could tell he was getting all the use he wanted out of Aileen.

I was like a conscientious kid with the family car. I never used it when the old man wanted it, and I always brought it home in as good condition as I took it out, with gas in the tank and air in the tires.

I suppose it must go without saying that I stopped picking up odd jobs on the days when Gregor didn't need me. When it came to a choice between slipping cents-off coupons under doors or slipping fingers into Aileen, it was the world's easiest decision for me to make.

I also stopped helping out in the darkroom. I think Gregor was surprised, but I let him get the impression that I was losing interest in photography as a lifetime career. Since he didn't pay me for help, he couldn't really bitch about it very strenuously.

I had never gotten around to finding out about getting my diploma by going to night school, and of course I couldn't really do anything about it at that time of the year, it being the middle of the term, but I had planned to find out what I had to find out and write away to Upper Valley for transcripts of my record so that I could start taking courses during the summer session. I didn't bother doing any of this, and when I thought about night school at all, I more or less thought in terms of starting in the fall instead of rushing things.

And I stopped going to the library as often as I had, and I stopped wandering around Chicago looking for women, and what it came down to, really, is that if I wasn't working or sleeping or sitting around with Gregor and Aileen, then I was in bed with her. Those were just about the only four choices during that period of time.

I spent some money on clothes, and I bought things like new shoelaces and a nail file and like that, but even without working the other jobs I was saving money. I would earn between forty and fifty a week helping Gregor, and my room and board cost me twenty, and I still didn't eat lunch, and it wasn't at all hard to save fifteen or twenty dollars out of each week's earnings, especially because I never left the house unless I had to. There was really no way for me to spend money, so I saved it.

This meant that by the end of May I had almost two hundred dollars, including the fifty for the modeling session. And because the money was accumulating with no strain at all I had the feeling that I was really getting somewhere and really making the kind of progress I had sworn I would make that first night at the Eagle Hotel.

When I think back on it now I wonder if maybe all of that sex was rotting my brain, because if there was one thing I wasn't doing, it was getting ahead in the world. Not in any way at all. I mean, a good long look at the pattern my life had taken would make Horatio Alger throw up.

Instead of a job with a future, I was, let's face it, working as sidekick to the world's most pathetic photographer. That's what he was, really. Taking candid pictures of morons on State Street and every few months making a big score by selling dirty pictures of his wife. And the dumbest part of it was that he worked harder for less money than if he'd been swinging a pick on a road gang, for Pete's sake. He took risks and put in long hours on his feet and just took nickels and dimes out of the street photography business. The dirty pictures made his real income, and he would have to space out the cash over a period of several months until Mark called him up and asked for more.

Now and then I wondered why he didn't go into the dirty picture business in a bigger way, hiring a variety of models and finding a way to distribute the pictures and making some real money. Not that I think being a pornographer is the best way to sail through life, but if you're going to be one anyway, why not be a successful one? It seems to me that if a girl is going to be a whore, she might as well be an expensive one. Right? So if Gregor had been the Kingpin of Filth in Chicago, or if he at least *tried* to be the Kingpin, I would have respected him. Or if he was a complete bum who just tried to coast along on the least possible amount of work, that would have at least made sense. But he wasn't lazy and he wasn't ambitious either, and this was the guy I was working for, this was the man teaching me his trade.

I mean, how stupid can you be?

I had wanted to save money, and I was saving it, but I was making, say, fifty dollars a week and saving twenty, and at the rate I was going, in twenty years I would still be making fifty a week and still saving twenty, and if you save twenty dollars a week, it will take you approximately a thousand years of steady work to save a million dollars.

(This is figured without what the savings-bank ads call The Miracle Of Compound Interest. According to them, if you put your money in a savings account you can't help winding up rich. I remember seeing a billboard telling what Washington's silver dollar would be worth today if he had put it in the bank. The figure was something ridiculously high, so I got a book from the library on coin collecting to find out what the same dollar would have been worth if Washington had *kept* it, and it turned out he would have been better off. But for all the good it did Washington he was even better off throwing it across the river. Or in it. So much for The Miracle Of Compound Interest.)

The thing is, I wasn't making real progress, and I wasn't looking for a real opportunity. And it was the same with my sex life, if you stopped to think about it, which most of the time I didn't. Because while I was having all this pleasure I was still as much a virgin as ever, and I wasn't coming any closer to not being a virgin. In fact I was actually locking myself out of any chance of losing my virginity, the same way I was keeping myself from any chance of getting a job with a future. See, I was getting satisfied with what I had with Aileen, and in the same way I was getting satisfied with that stupid job and everything else.

That was one thing about the kids in the Horatio Alger books. They were never satisfied. No matter how well things started shaping up, they had the decency to go on wanting more and more and more. So they kept pushing, and whenever opportunity knocked they ran to the door and answered it. If opportunity knocked on my door I never would have heard it because I would have been too busy putting blurry yellow cards in people's hands or putting my own blurry little hands on Aileen.

Not that I had these thoughts all the time. That was the worst of it—that I didn't. That I was content with the way things were going. Take a man who is content with what he does and the way he lives and what have you got?

A happy man, obviously.

But that's not exactly right, either, because I wasn't really contented, because I didn't have what I wanted. I was settling for less, that's what I was doing. I was having little off-in-left-field climaxes with Aileen when what I really wanted to do was slide into home plate. I was getting by in a dumb job when I really wanted to get ahead. And no matter how comfortable that couch was when Aileen was on it with me, and no matter how often that happened, sooner or later I would have to be bothered by the way things were going.

On Memorial Day, a veteran sold me a poppy. He stuck that poppy into my hand just as neatly as I had learned to stick the yellow cards into the jerks' hands, and I took it like any other jerk, only I couldn't just drop it on the ground and keep walking. Or maybe I could have done this, but then he would have been within his rights if he brained me with his crutch. I gave him a quarter and he said something about the Last Of The Big Spenders. I stuck the stupid poppy in my buttonhole. That way at least I didn't have to buy another one.

But when I walked another block, it hit me that I was more a cripple than the guy who sold me the poppy. I don't know how I made the connection. It came in one quick flash and once I had it I couldn't let go of it. I kept seeing myself with a leg missing, lurching through life like that.

And I couldn't stick around with an image like that in my mind.

I waited until the weekend was over. The Sunday paper was filled with want ads, and I bought it and sat in a diner and went through it, and I found what I wanted. It wasn't a job with a future, either, but it was one that would take me out of Chicago, and I had enough sense to know that I couldn't stay in Chicago if I wanted to get out of the tender trap I was in. I had to travel, and then I could concentrate on Getting Ahead and all the rest of it.

Monday was a work day, but I took a long lunch hour, and during that lunch hour I went over and applied for the job. And got it. (No big deal—you had to have two heads or something for them to turn you down. They were easier to get into than the Army. More later.)

And Monday night, after old Gregor went night-night, I did everything possible to score with Aileen. I tried to break those silly rules of hers and get something straight between us once and for all, and as usual it didn't work. I had more or less fixed up a game in my mind, making a bargain with myself that if I laid her I would stay in Chicago but if I didn't I would go. I gave it the old Upper Valley try and when it didn't work I took Aileen's motherly advice to behave myself and be a good boy and make sweet love with her. I got on top of her and rubbed the two of us together in a way we had both grown to enjoy no end. I made sweet love all over her stomach and she danced off to wash away the sweet love I had made, and she pecked my cheek and told me I was her sweet baby and to sleep tight, and she went into her bedroom and got back in bed with the State Street Shutterbug.

I got dressed in the dark and put my extra clothes and stuff in a paper bag. I thought about leaving a note, but I couldn't think of anything that wasn't either hopelessly corny or slightly nasty, and I didn't want to be either. I told myself I would write her a letter someday. You can tell yourself things like that as often as you want and it doesn't cost you a thing.

I sat up all night in different crummy diners, drinking so much coffee that I kept shaking and peeing and shaking and peeing. I was downtown in plenty of time to catch my ride in the morning, and when our car left the city limits of Chicago it wasn't even noon yet.

So that was three months, and my $27.46 had turned into $191.80, which is better than it could have done through The Miracle Of Compound Interest. And I had spent more time on third base than Ron Santo.

That toddling town.

CHAPTER SIX

WHEN I RANG THE DOORBELL, THE CHIMES played the first two bars of a hymn. I couldn't tell you which one. I stood there patiently, wanting to ring it again but holding off, and eventually I heard the pitter-patter of little old feet. I timed myself so that I was whipping off my little blue-visored cap just as she was opening the door.

She wasn't the girl of my dreams. When you are young enough and horny enough (like me, Chip Harrison, for instance) you can't even open a Coke bottle without hoping there will be a beautiful girl in it. And on this job I kept waiting for the time one of the doors would be opened by a Neglected Young Housewife, or a Wanton Suburban College

Girl Home From School, or an Off-Duty Whore. And instead the doors kept being opened by women who stopped thinking about sex the day Hayes beat Tilden.

This one must have gone to school with Tilden's grandmother, from the looks of her. She was a tiny wrinkled little lady with bright eyes the color of frostbitten lips. Her face cracked into a smile.

She looked up at me and said, "Yes, young man? You've come for the bake sale donation, haven't you?"

I said I was afraid I hadn't, and I went into a little explanation of who I was and why I had turned up on her doorstep. While I talked I held my cap in both hands and squeezed it in and out of shape. I didn't do this because I was nervous. That's just the way it was supposed to look, because according to old Flickinger the more nervous and earnest you seemed the more trustworthy you were, at least as far as old ladies were concerned.

It was hard to look nervous without doing the little bit of business with the cap, because I actually delivered my set piece without even paying attention to what I was saying. I might as well have been a record player. While my mouth got all the words out, my mind thought about how little this woman had in common with the girl of my dreams, and that I might have guessed as much, because nymphomaniacs don't go out of their way to have chimes that play hymns—at least most of them don't—and while I didn't recognize that tune, it certainly wasn't "Roll Me Over in the Clover."

"—free inspection with no obligation whatsoever," I finished up, and gave my cap a final twist, and hung my head just the littlest bit, because you couldn't go overboard and look too pathetic or you got tons of warm milk and cookies shoved down your throat.

"*Rowrbazzle*," she said.

That seemed like a funny thing for anybody to say, let alone Tilden's grandmother here, but then of course I saw that she wasn't the one who said it. It was her cat. He was standing next to her, and he was as big for a cat as she was small for an old lady. He was built like a Siamese, with a blackish-brown coat and horrible yellow eyes. I always liked cats, but then they had always said sensible things like *Meow*. This was the first one that had ever said anything like *Rowrbazzle* within my hearing and I wasn't sure just how I felt about it. It put me off stride a little, if you really want to know.

"Now just one moment, young man," she said.

The woman this time. "You wait right here, and I won't be a minute. You wait now."

I waited. So did the cat. Now would have been a good time for me to step inside and let the screen door close behind me, which was the recommended procedure at this stage of the game. Whoever had worked up the recommended procedure had never met a cat that said *Rowrbazzle*. I stayed where I was, and old Rowrbazzle stayed where he was, and the screen door was the Demilitarized Zone.

Then the old lady came back, and I slapped my smile back in place and whipped off my cap again, and then I noticed what she had in both her little liver-spotted hands.

What she had was an old dueling pistol that was almost as big as her dippy old cat. Her hands were shaking, and the pistol was bobbing up and down like a red red robin, and it was pointing at me, and it looked as though it might go off at any moment.

I said, "Hey! Hey, hang on a minute!"

"This weapon is loaded and primed, young man."

"I believe it."

"And let me assure you that it works perfectly well. It is old, but age is not always detrimental. This pistol is in full possession of its faculties."

I was sure it was. I was perfectly willing to believe that it was still every bit as good as it was the day Aaron Burr shot Alexander Hamilton with it.

"You don't understand," I said.

"You will leave this block of houses at once, young man. You will leave directly. The people on this block are all good Christians."

"You don't under—"

"Except for the young woman in Number One-twenty-one," she said her voice quavering. "She is a Methodist, and I believe her husband is a wine drinker or worse. You may stop there if you wish. I would not advise it. Last September a boy a bit older than you examined that young woman's furnace and took it all apart and refused to repair it unless he was paid. I doubt she'd let you into her house after an experience of that sort, but you may try if you wish. I've enough on my mind without protecting Methodists, and them wine drinkers in the bargain. Not that I know for a fact that she drinks with him, but they flock together, you know. And I thought you had come about the bake sale. You have an innocent face in sheep's clothing. Read the Book of Ezekiel."

"*Rowrbazzle.*"

"Calvin dislikes you, young man. Our animals can sense things which we can only discover through reasoning. I am going to count ten, and if you are not off my property by the time I reach ten, I will shoot you. I do not hold with violence, but the Lord protects those who look to their own protection. Read the third chapter of the Second Samuel. One. Two. Three. Four—"

I scrambled down the porch steps and between two rows of private hedge to the street, expecting a musket ball to come tearing into me at any moment. The only reason it didn't was that I was well out of the way before her tinny old voice got to ten. Otherwise she would have shot me. No question about it, she would have blown my god-damned head off without thinking twice about it. If Calvin said *Rowrbazzle* to you, you just didn't stand a chance around there.

I passed up all the houses on that block. Even the lady in Number 121, the Methodist. I didn't care if she was a Sun Worshipper. I wasn't taking any chances.

Around the corner I almost collided with Jimmy Joe. He started to tell me he had just written out an order, but I cut in and told him about Calvin and *Rowrbazzle* and Grandma Tilden. "Oh, that's nothing," he said airily. "I've had more guns pointed at me than fingers. They never shoot."

"This one would have."

"Ninety-nine times out of a hundred the guns aren't even loaded. These people keep unloaded guns around just to put guys like you and me uptight. And the average person, especially a lady, they couldn't hit a barn from inside of it."

"This gun was loaded, and she would have shot, and she wouldn't have missed."

"Yeah, sure. Prove it."

"Okay," I said. I was still having trouble catching my breath. "Okay, smart ass. You go up on the porch and give her a pitch and see if she shoots you or not. I'll bet you ten bucks you get shot."

"It's a sucker bet for you. If she shoots me, how do you collect?"

"I'll take my chances."

He laughed. When he did this, it always reminded me of a big old boxer who belonged to one of the masters at a school I went to in Connecticut. That dog barked just about like that. "Forget it," Jimmy Joe said. "The important question is did she call the cops."

"I don't think she would. Never even threatened to. She's the vigilante type."

"That's all to the good."

"But I'm not supposed to go on that block because of all the God-fearing Christians. And one Methodist."

"Methodists are Christians."

"You want to go tell her? If Flick wants me I'll be working the next block over."

"They're all new houses."

"How's the one after that?"

"Better."

"Then that's where I'll be. Luck."

"Up yours," he agreed. "And watch out for the Christians."

"Right, and you watch out for the Lions."

I didn't meet any more old ladies with dueling pistols that afternoon, or any cats named Calvin with weird vocabularies. I did meet a whole lot of people who had no trouble closing the door in the middle of my pitch.

I had always thought that was about the most aggravating thing that could happen to someone working door to door, getting a door slammed in your face. It can be sort of jarring the first couple dozen times it happens, but I'll tell you something, once you get used to it you learn to welcome it. Not that you set out looking to get doors closed on you, but if you're going to strike out anyway, which is going to happen ninety-nine times out of a hundred to the greatest salesman who ever lived, you might as well strike out as soon as possible.

The less time you waste on the stiffs, the more calls you can make in a given period of time. And the more calls you make, the more sales you make, and that's gospel. Old Flickinger says he'd rather have a chimpanzee who makes a hundred calls a day than a genius who makes fifty. Good old Flick.

"I been on the road for thirty years and more, kid, and if I learned one thing it's you don't lose money by ringing doorbells. And if there's one word of advice I can give you it's never get into any woman's pants without she signs on the dotted line. Once you got the order written it's another story. With the sale made you can afford half an hour in the kip, even an hour if you like the broad's style. But without you get the order there's no percentage. You just waste time you can't afford, and then all she wants to do is get you out of there without she buys anything, or else she keeps you around and gives you coffee and dangles it in front of you that maybe she'll buy, and you wind up going another round in the kip, and you waste the whole fucking afternoon without you get any order at all. Now maybe you'll give her a kiss or a feel to set up a sale, on the lines of what you might call a free sample, but that's all. If there's one word of advice I can give you that's it."

Good old Flick. The first time I heard that little speech I saw myself giving in gracefully to one woman after the next, and doing so well in bed with them that I got order after order, and— Well, there's no big suspense to keep up, since Francine wasn't in the picture yet and you know I was still as pure as Ivory Soap when I met her, so let's just say that it wasn't like that at all in the door-to-door game, at least not for me, and while Flick's advice might have been sound, I wasn't getting a chance to put it into practice.

As I said, I got doors closed in my face, and I also got the usual percentage of dimwits who felt sorry enough for me to let me give them the whole speech, but who didn't feel sorry enough for me to let me sell them anything. And then just before it was time to quit I hooked a gray-haired lady who lived all alone in a Victorian house that must have had a hundred rooms in it. She had a cat, but it said what any normal cat says. She said its name was Featherfoot, and that it was a boy but she had had it fixed. She said it so daintily that I almost asked what had been wrong with it. She also had had it declawed so it wouldn't ruin the furniture. She might have gone all the way and had it stuffed so that it wouldn't go to the bathroom and to cut down on the cost of feeding it. If

I ever have a cat, which I probably won't, since it's hard enough to keep myself in sardines, let alone two of us, I would let it keep its claws and its balls intact. I mean, if you don't want the complete animal, I don't think you should have any of it. I mean, how would you like it if you were a cat and they did *that* to you?

That's getting off the subject, but so did this old lady. She went on and on about one thing or another. She had lost her husband a year ago, she told me. I was sort of listening to every third word out of her mouth, so I thought at first that she must have lost him in one of the hundred rooms in that old barn. But of course she meant he was dead. I hate people who don't like to say certain words, so they say that the cat is fixed when they mean castrated, or that their husband is lost when they mean he's dead as a doornail.

She kept on talking, and I went around the house on a tour of inspection, and she droned on about how much trouble there was in keeping up a house when you were a woman all alone in the world. I knew I had her then. I worked my way around the back of the house until I found a spot where there were traces of sawdust on the concrete, and I whipped out my magnifying glass and made clucking noises.

"Oh, dear," she said. "Oh, land's sake."

I pointed to the sawdust. "See that?" I said.

She saw it and started apologizing for never having noticed it before. I developed a sudden thirst and asked her if she thought I might be able to have a glass of water. When she came back with the water, I showed her a test tube half full of the little rascals. She almost spilled the water.

"Oh, dear. And you captured all of them while I was in the house?"

"That's right. There are some of the ones I missed. See, there they go."

She looked, *tsstssing* unhappily as the little devils scurried madly over the clapboard siding. That was always the real convincer. Even the most gullible person could look at the ones in the test tube and still figure his house was safe. There was always the hope in their minds that I had picked up the last of them. And the suspicious ones might point out that I could have brought the test tube along with me. But when they saw those termites actually burrowing into their own house it got them where they lived. No joke, it really did.

We went in the house and I filled out the service agreement and got her to sign it. She didn't even ask what the job was going to cost until after I had the agreement folded and tucked away. I said that the price would depend upon the extent of infestation, and that our costs were nominal, and that all our work was guaranteed. This didn't answer her question but she didn't ask again, so I guess she thought she was satisfied.

Before I could get out of there she asked to see the termites again. I gave her the tube. "Nasty nasty vicious things," she said, with all the hate in the world in her voice. And wouldn't you know that she insisted on taking the tube outside and spilling the devils out onto the sidewalk and then divebombing the living shit out of them with a can of spray insect killer. "Die die die," she said, and the poor little critters curled up and did just that.

It was a nuisance, but no real harm done. Flickinger had a five-gallon pickle jug swarming with the little bastards, and it wasn't that much trouble to get a tubeful of them. A pain in the neck, that's all.

That night I sat around the motel after I refilled the test tube. Jimmy Joe and Keegan were at a movie I hadn't wanted to see. Lester went off without saying where, probably to look for queers at the bus station. He liked girls and his suitcase was half full of pictures of naked women, but queers were always easier to find, even in the fifth largest city in Indiana, which is where we happened to be just then. You could jump off the top of the tallest building in the fifth largest city in Indiana without doing much more than spraining your ankle, but for our crew this was considered a pretty big city. We worked towns you honestly wouldn't believe. We went all through Illinois and Indiana, and sometimes the towns were so small that Lester had to find himself the one queer in the town, or what you might call the town's faggot in residence. But he always seemed to connect.

The reason I could tolerate old Lester was that he had a reasonable attitude about what he did. He didn't run on and on about it and he didn't bug you with a lot of details you'd be a lot happier not knowing, but at the same time he wasn't one of those nerds who did it on the sly, like my old roommate Haskell who tried to pretend his cock and his hand had never even been introduced to one another, for Pete's sake. If you asked him a question he'd answer it, but if you left it alone he'd keep quiet. This made him relatively easy to take.

As far as Lester was concerned there was nothing revolting about going with a queer. The only thing shameful about it was that it would be a lot better and more satisfying with a girl. But he didn't figure it made him queer to be with a queer. Not that Lester is the first person on earth to ever come up with this line of thought. But it seems to me, if you happen to care, that when two men had sex together they were both queer and it didn't make a hell of a difference which one was down on his knees. It wasn't as though Lester was just phoning in his part of the deal. But whether you wanted to consider him queer or not (and if you did it wasn't a good idea to tell him about it), I got along fine with him.

See, that's one of the fringe benefits of selling termite extermination service door to door. You become very tolerant of people.

Anyhow, I was less interested in accompanying Lester to the bus station than in seeing the movie with Keegan and Jimmy Joe. There was one other member of the crew, a recently divorced ex-Marine named Solly, who was inclined to have much better luck with women than the rest of us. He was having some of that luck right now in his motel room. And Flickinger, the crew leader, was doing what he always did after sunset. What he did involved a bottle and a glass. He never minded company, but if you were going to sit with him he expected you to drink with him, and even without trying to match him shot for shot I was in big trouble, because if I took a short drink for every three long ones of his I would still be drunk in an hour and sick for the next day and a half. One drink of Gregor's lousy brandy was all right, but I wasn't ready to handle anything like a whole night of serious drinking.

Besides, as I discovered the second of the two times I had kept Flick company, he never remembered in the morning just what he had said the night before. He never said anything particularly weird either of the times I was with him, and he behaved the same as he did when he was cold sober—he never took a drink before the sun went down, or passed one up after it did—but the thing of it was that he wouldn't know one night that he had told you certain stories on an earlier night, and anecdotes that are fairly lively the first time around get a little stale the second time.

And if you tried to tell Flick that you'd heard such and such a story before, he argued with you.

So I didn't go to Flick's room, and of course I didn't go to Solly's room, and the other three guys were out somewhere, and I didn't have anything to read, and Flick owned the only car and had let Jimmy Joe and Keegan borrow it, which didn't really enter into it since I couldn't drive anyway.

Well, I mean I know how, but they get agitated if they catch you driving without a license, and I never got one.

So there was nothing to do and no place to go, and that gave this particular evening a whole lot in common with most of the evenings I'd spent since I left Chicago.

Unless you happened to work on one of those traveling sales crews, you probably don't know what they're like. I didn't have the faintest idea myself until I was actually hired and on the job. The arrangement was simple enough. The crew consisted of five guys anywhere from eighteen on up (well, I lied) and a crew leader. You would be assigned a certain territory, which in our case was eastern Illinois and western Indiana, and within that territory you would go wherever the crew boss decided and stay as long as it was worthwhile. The crew leader took care of all your regular expenses—hotel, meals, car expenses, and so on—and got reimbursed by the company.

For every sale you made, the salesman got twenty-five dollars and the crew leader got fifteen. The crew leader did his own selling too and got to keep the whole forty bucks on his own sales. (Flick's percentage was officially a secret, but it was one of the first things he told you when he sat drinking with you.)

The point is that if you made a sale you wound up with twenty-five bucks free and clear, since you didn't have any living expenses at all. If you sold one lousy exterminating job a day, you could salt away better than five hundred dollars a month. And on the other hand if you had a terrible day or a terrible week or even a terrible month, you never had to worry about missing meals or being locked out of your room, because your basic expenses were always taken care of.

I just read through that last paragraph, and it sounds as good now as it did when I first heard it. Because I haven't mentioned the one thing they didn't stress, either.

Which is that you go out as a crew for a three-month tour, and you don't collect nickel number one until you finish the tour. It wasn't hard to figure out why they did it this way. See, the system was based on the idea of five men and a crew boss, which was the best size group from an economic standpoint. And if two or three of those men decided to call it quits while the crew was working off in East Crayfish or Fort Dingbat, the whole crew stopped being a profitable deal for the company. But if a guy had to go back at the end of the hitch to collect his money, that tended to discourage him from quitting.

Of course you would still be entitled to your pay whether you quit or not. But being entitled didn't mean anybody was going to hand the money to you.

Or, in Flick's words, "Any of youse quits without the three months are up, you just kissed your dough good-bye. And if I ever catches youse again, you can kiss your ass good-bye, too, because I'll kick it clear to Wausau County for you."

I don't know where the hell Wausau County is.

According to Keegan, who had been working what he called the Bug Game on and off for almost five years, there was another reason why they didn't pay you until your shift was done. They had to confirm the signatures. Otherwise the salesmen could just write up a couple of phony orders every day, knock down a couple of hundred dollars a week, and spend all their time watching television.

"And there are some that would do just that," he told me, with a wink. "You wouldn't believe it in a fine upstanding business like this one, Chip my lad, but there are hordes of dishonest people in this world."

I believed it.

Not that I had ever had any grave doubts on

that score. But in the time I spent showing poor widow ladies my little plastic tube full of termites, I learned more about how people could be crooked without going to jail than I ever knew existed. One thing that I couldn't get out of my head was that my parents must have been real hard-core criminals. Up until then I always figured that they couldn't have been so bad if they went all their lives without getting sent to jail, but now I saw that I had been looking at it the wrong way around. If they had actually gotten themselves to a point where it looked as though they just might have to go to jail, then they were obviously a pretty criminal pair, old Mom and Dad, because you can be crooked enough to pull corks out of wine bottles with your toes and never see a cop except to say hello to, or fix a traffic ticket.

I already knew that nobody seemed to pay any attention to the law, or at least not in the way the law had in mind. In Chicago, for instance, you couldn't do commercial street photography, and even if you did you couldn't pass out handbills that way, because that constitutes an invitation to litter and means you're creating a nuisance. All of which meant that Gregor gave the patrolman on his beat ten dollars a week and never heard any more about it.

(I had always known things like this went on, but I thought, you know, that it was strictly Big Time Criminals who got involved in them. Not some plodding clod like Gregor, for Pete's sake. And I knew some cops took graft, and how it's a big temptation and all, but to take ten dollars? A rotten ten dollars from a simp like Gregor?)

Well, this happens in more places than Chicago. In every city or town our crew went to, there was a man Flickinger called the Fixer. The Fixer might be somebody in the police department or sheriff's office, or it might be a politician, or it might be some lawyer or businessman who was in good with the local government. And whoever the particular fixer might be, Flick would tell him he was bringing in a door-to-door crew and he wanted to have all the red tape handled in advance, like the permits or licenses or whatever was needed, and without the bother of filling out a lot of forms. And then Flick would slip the Fixer an envelope, and the Fixer would talk to whoever had to be talked to, and he'd keep part of what was in the envelope and pass on the rest, and none of us would have to worry about any aggravation from the police. And I don't mean just that they wouldn't give us a hard time about not having licenses. Besides that, there was always the fact that a certain number of noncustomers would call the cops and complain about us for one reason or another. But the word would be out, and when those calls came in the cop who answered the phone would say *Yeah* and *Sure, ma'am* and listen while all the information came over the wire and into his ear, but he wouldn't bother writing any of it down, and we would never even hear about it, unless maybe someone would call Flick privately and ask him to for Christ's sake ask his boys to be a little more diplomatic in their dealings with the natives.

Don't ask how much was in the envelope. One of the reasons Flick got that fifteen dollars a sale extra was that he knew what it would take to fix each particular fixer.

I went out into the hall and got a Coke out of the machine. I was leaning against the wall drinking it when Solly came out of his room with a plastic pitcher. He carried it to the ice machine and filled it up.

I said, "Heavy night?"

"All she wants to do is drink and screw. I wouldn't mind, only she drinks better'n she screws."

"Did you ask her if she's got a friend?"

"If she had a friend, I'd take the friend and boot this one out on her hinder. She's a pig. You, Chip, you got the right idea."

"I do?"

"Goddamn right."

He seemed to be more than a little looped. I said, "What's the right idea? Coca-Cola?"

"Not Coca-fuckin'-Cola. It's bad for your teeth, you know that?"

"Not if you use a regular bottle opener."

"Huh?" He blinked. "Smart ass. But you got the right idea. The girls I see you out with."

"Oh."

"Whattaya mean, *oh*?" Solly became very forceful when he drank. Not belligerent or nasty, just emphatic. "Decent girls, pretty girls. And I never see you with the same girl twice. Smart. The right idea."

He weaved away and plunged back to his room and woman while I tried to think of an answer. Not that it was worth the trouble. The girls he had seen me out with were nice decent girls, all right. And pretty girls. And I guess I was getting a little better at knowing what to say to them and how to make time with them, because these weren't girls that anybody introduced me to, and they weren't girls who went out looking to get picked up. They were ordinary run-of-the-mill nice small-town girls that I would meet during the job or at a restaurant and that I would take to a movie and out for coffee or something like that.

If you can convince someone to sign a piece of paper agreeing to let Dynamic Termite Extermination, Inc. rid his house of termites and dendivorous vermin (that's what it said on the paper they signed, and you can look it up in your Funk and Wagnall's) for whatever fee DTE, Inc. wanted to charge, if you can do all that, you really ought to be able to convince some small-town girl to go to a movie with you.

But not to anything much more dynamic than a movie, as it happens.

I drank a second soft drink, but this time I made it an Uncola, probably because I was brainwashed by Solly telling me Coke would ruin my teeth. It probably would, but the Uncola probably would, too.

Because I was beginning to come to the conclusion that everything was a con.

Which is a hell of a conclusion to come to, for Pete's sake, especially when you happen to be descended from a long line of con men. Well, two of them anyway. And when you've decided to become a success along legitimate lines and to work hard and save your money and marry the boss's daughter and do all the other things right, too.

Why go through all that if some smooth-talking little rat could come along and stand on your stoop and twist his cap in his hands and wind up costing you a couple of hundred dollars to kill termites that weren't there to begin with, and that wouldn't hurt your house a whole lot even if they were? (Because this may be something you never thought of, in which case I'm going to be saving you a lot of money over the years, because the first thing we all learned is that maybe ninety-nine houses out of a hundred have some termites, and those houses will go on standing for a couple of hundred years without anybody doing anything about those termites. See, it takes a long time for a termite to eat a house. It even takes a long time for a lot of termites to eat a house. But you take the average idiot and show him a termite eating his house, and he figures that in another week there won't be anything left but the foundation.

(And while I'm on the subject, the second thing we all learned was that you couldn't in a million years sell an extermination job to somebody with a brick house. Flick said you can't sell them fire-proofing, either, and Flick would know; he's sold everything at one time or another, and if that includes his mother and his sister I wouldn't be surprised. But people who have brick houses seem to think the brick is what holds the house together, so—

(You know, I have the feeling that I might be telling you more about termites than you really want to know. Maybe all of this will get cut out before the book gets printed, or maybe the book won't ever *get* printed, which would mean rough sledding for one Chip Harrison, but either way I'm going to cool it at this point with all this inside information about the termite business. That's a firm promise.

(In fact, I'm going to cool it on that forgettable evening, as far as that goes, because it wasn't the kind of evening you would want to read about. I rapped a little with Lester when he came in, and I let Jimmy Joe tell me the plot of the movie he and Keegan saw. And I made up a lie about having a girl in my room and banging her while they were at the movie, and Jimmy Joe made up a lie about picking up a girl after the movie. We were both lying and knew it, but it broke the monotony in a small way. And outside of having a couple more soft drinks and reading an Indianapolis newspaper—which made the *Chicago Tribune* seem like the *Daily Worker*, or close to it—that was all there was to that evening, so there's no point wasting every-body's time with it.

(It was the night after that one that might inter-est you, when Solly brought the redhead back to the motel and organized a gang bang. I have to admit it was more interesting than Cokes and Un-colas. And it did more damage than any termites I ever saw.)

CHAPTER SEVEN

DURING THE DAY I HAD BEEN WORKING the same area where I'd made a sale the day before. Up until then the television weatherman had been saying it was unseasonably cool for mid-July, which meant it was reasonably comfortable. But that day it decided to get seasonable again.

I'm writing this on a cold damp rotten morning. My radiator is some slumlord's idea of decoration, completely nonfunctional. But I can get warm just remembering that day. I didn't make a sale. No one did. No one expected to. I think I worked as long as anyone, and I was back in my air-conditioned room by three-thirty. Flickinger didn't even put in a token gripe. Pointless. We could have sold air conditioners or dry ice or Japanese fans, but that was about the extent of it. It was so hot we didn't even talk about how hot it was, if that makes sense.

I skipped dinner and stretched out on my bed in my shorts and let the air conditioner blow on me. I woke up shivering, figure that one out, when Lester banged on my door. I let him in and he flopped in a chair and waited for his breath to come back. He had gone out for dinner and walked through all that heat, and looking at him made me glad I stayed around the room instead.

We talked about this and that, one thing and the other, and ultimately reached Topic A. I launched into a long story that was kind of loosely based on something that happened with Aileen, except that in this version of the story we didn't worry about being faithful to Gregor, who was a Cuban refugee dentist in the latest version. I don't know if Lester believed it or not. I don't think he cared enough to worry whether it was true or not. When you sit around swapping sex stories to keep from dying of boredom, nobody really gives a shit if they're true or not. Just so they're sufficiently interesting and/or horny to keep you awake.

"You know something?" he demanded, when I had carried Carmelita and myself to the heights of rapture. "When all is said and done, no woman really knows how to give head."

I made a noncommittal noise.

"You agree with me, Chip?"

I said something that sounded like *Rowrbazzle*. Because it was one of those questions like *Have you stopped beating your meat?* Whatever you said, you came off either more ignorant or more informed than you might want to.

Lester talked for a while, sort of saying but not saying that he was afraid he got more of a kick out of the queers than he wanted to, and hinting that if he did have a woman available on a steady basis he might miss the Greyhound Terminal set, water on the knee and all. I just made grunting sounds, which was all the situation called for. One thing I've noticed is that when you want to talk something out and get it right in your mind, all you really want the other person to do is be there with his mouth shut. It's a way of talking to yourself without feeling a little flaky about it.

He dropped the subject when Jimmy Joe came in unannounced and stuck his head in front of the air conditioner.

"Hey," he wanted to know, "am I interrupting anything?"

"We were talking about sex," Lester said.

"That's the trouble. Everybody talks about it and nobody does anything about it." And he sat down on the carpet and joined the party.

Bit by bit they all filtered in. Keegan first, and then Flickinger himself, standing at the door with a stupid look on his face and a bottle of gin in each hand. He came in and said he felt like company, and why didn't we all join him in a drink? No one could think of a reason not to. We drank gin on the rocks out of water tumblers. Keegan smacked his lips, wrinkled his nose, frowned, and said he wanted a little less vermouth next time around.

That reminded Flick of a story. I knew it would, because I had heard the story twice before, the two times I got drunk with him. Every last one of us had heard that goddamned story but nobody wanted to ruin his evening by saying anything about it.

You know, somewhere in this world Flickinger must have a drinking buddy who has the same kind of memory as Flick does. And I can just imagine the two of them sitting up night after night, lapping up the sauce and telling each other the exact same stories every single night. And each time Flick would think he was telling the story for the first time, and each time the other juicehead would think he was hearing it for the first time, and the two of them would go on and on, repeating like a decimal until the world came to an end.

Flick finished his story, finally, and poured everybody another drink whether they needed it or not, and got that look on his face that let you know another story was on its way. Before he could get his mouth in gear, Keegan said, "Why isn't Solly at our little party?"

He wasn't looking for an answer. He just wanted to throw a question in Flickinger's way. But no sooner were the words out than the door flew open, and there, drunker than the five of us put together, was Solly himself.

"Well, it's about time," he said. "Wondered where you all went to. Knocked on this door and that door and thought you were all gone, and you're all here. Goddamn good thing, too. Never forgive yourselves if you missed this."

"Somebody give him a drink," Lester suggested.

"Brought you boys a present," Solly said. He stuck out his hand and just left it hanging there, waiting for someone to put a drink in it as Lester had suggested, but that's the trouble with indefinite orders; we all waited for somebody else to give Solly a drink, and Solly's hand just stayed out in the air for a little while before he remembered where he had left it and brought it back.

"A present," he repeated, and got his hand back, and stuck it out into the hallway and brought it back in again, only now there was a girl's wrist in it, with a girl attached. A redhead with a see-through sleeveless blouse and a flaring white miniskirt that ended less than an inch short of indecent exposure.

"This is Cherry," he said, and started to laugh. "Jesus Christ in Marlboro Country, but if this here is cherry then I'm an unkey's moncle."

He tried to say it straight, and muffed it again, and fell apart laughing. Then he tried again from the beginning.

"This here is Cherry," he said. "Her name. She wants to get checked out for dendivorous insects. No, what she wants is to get laid and relayed and parlayed. Screwed, blewed, and tattooed. She wants to take on everybody who's game, and I thought of my old buddies, and I thought, shit, what else do you do for kicks when it's a hundred and ten in the shade?"

Cherry was just standing there with a simple smile on her face. I guess that was the only kind she was capable of. She did look simple. There was no getting around it. She looked great, with a face that was reasonably pretty even if you didn't fall heart-stoppingly in love with her, and with a body that would have made you willing to have her around even if the face had been horrible. But there was something in that face, some quality that was part stupidity and part vacancy, in the sense that if you opened up her head you would find a sign saying that part of her mind was on a sabbatical in Europe or something. So she stood there looking dumb and desirable, and that's exactly what she was.

The rest of us were saying encouraging things like *Hey* and *Wow* and *Sounds good* and *No crap*. And Solly put one of his hands on Cherry's little behind and gave kind of a shove, and she took four or five little running steps into the room. Solly followed her inside and closed the door.

"Now show the boys what you got there," he said. "Get your clothes off, Cherry. Hurry it up. Any of you bastards got a deck of cards? High goes first and so on in order, and the same order for seconds and thirds, and after that we'll worry about it."

"Seconds and thirds?"

"Look at her. How often do you get a shot at something like that? You guys, I don't know, you guys get so little ass that when you jerk off you close your eyes and pretend you're jerking off. You think one shot at Cherry here is going to be all you want? Jesus, *look* at her!"

I don't know who he was talking to, because I'm pretty sure we were all looking at her. It seemed to me that she looked awfully young, but that happens with simple people. They don't have the sense to worry about things.

She took everything off, and she stood there with the same smile on her face, and I thought, well, take a good look at this one, Chip, because this is the one you'll never forget, the first girl ever for you, and nothing can stop you now.

"Ace is high. Suits are spades high, then hearts, then diamonds and then clubs. Same as in bridge, but you bastards don't play bridge. Cut the cards, dammit."

Keegan wanted to cut first to determine the cutting order. Jimmy Joe told him to for Christ's sake save the comedy for some other time. Flickinger, for once in his life, wasn't reminded of a story. Lester looked as though they could tear down every Greyhound station and throw all the faggots on the fire and he wouldn't mind for a minute. Solly cut the pack and got the seven of clubs and said something appropriate. Keegan cut the jack of diamonds. Jimmy Joe got the jack of clubs and insisted that put him ahead of Keegan. Keegan told him to piss off. Solly said diamonds were ahead of clubs. Jimmy Joe told Solly to piss off. Flickinger was sitting on a chair next to Cherry. He had one hand on her behind and was stroking up along the inside of her thigh with the other.

I was going to get an ace. I knew it. I could feel it, the way sometimes you can feel things.

Lester cut a nine, it doesn't matter which suit. Flickinger was so busy with Cherry it was hard to get his attention, but finally he cut the cards and got the queen of hearts.

Solly said, "Son of a bitch, that puts him first. He gets fifteen bucks every time one of us makes a sale, and now he gets first crack at her crack."

"Wait a minute," someone said. "It's the kid's turn."

"Flick might as well start. Queen's gonna be high."

"Aces are higher than queens," I said. I gave the words a Dean Martin drawl because I felt just that cool and confident. I reached out for the pack of cards, cut, and got the fucking four of clubs. They all laughed their heads off, except for old Flick who was too busy getting his pants off.

Lester put a glass of gin in my hand. "No sweat," he said. "Somebody's gotta be last. Just five guys ahead of you. The condition everybody's in, you'll be in the saddle in fifteen minutes. If it takes that long."

"Shit," I said. I drank the gin in one swallow. I don't ever do that, not even with a normal sized drink, and this was a whole glass of gin. I had already swallowed it before I realized what I had done, and even then I didn't give a damn.

"A girl like this, she'll just be warming up when you get her."

"I'll bet."

"Look at her face. Jesus, look at the old bull socking it to her, and she just lies there with that grin on her face. Like she's enjoying herself but it isn't really reaching her. You get a girl like that who wants to pull a train, you'd think of her as basically hot, right? But look at her. Cool as ice. That's the thing. It takes her three or four men just to put her in the mood. God almighty, but will you look at Flickinger. I didn't know he had it in him. Hung like a stud horse, too. If she can't feel what he's throwing her she must have a bun full of novocaine. He's gonna ruin her for the rest of us if he don't hurry up and get it over with."

"He'll ruin her for the entire human race," someone else said. "She won't be fit for anything but donkeys and horses. Take it easy, Flick!"

"And get it over with, Flick, you mother!"

Flickinger got it over with, and almost got himself over with in the process. He finished roaring, and collapsed on the girl, and whether it was the sex or the liquor or what I don't know, but he went out like a light. We had to roll him off of her, and Keegan kept saying that he was probably dead, but he wasn't. We got him into a chair and let him sit there by himself while Keegan took over for him.

Somebody handed me the bottle. I knew what I was doing this time, but all the same I took a drink. Just a short one, though. Not that I was afraid I wouldn't be able to do anything. I knew I would be able to do anything I wanted to do. But what worried me was that I might be like Flickinger and have a blackout. If I finally got laid after all this time and then couldn't even remember it, for Pete's sake, I might as well kill myself.

I wondered if Flickinger would remember. Maybe he just forgot telling stories to people. I looked around to make sure he was okay. He was conscious now, but his breath was coming along pretty raggedly.

While Keegan gave her a slow rhythmic banging, the rest of us somehow automatically started taking off our own clothes. We didn't say anything but just did this. I suppose the idea was that we were getting ready so that no time would be lost, but it didn't make any real sense for me, for example, to be in such a mad rush to get out of my clothes when there were still four men who were going to have her before my turn came.

What it was, I suppose, was that we were all knocked out enough by the heat and the air conditioning and the sexual excitement of the scene that the usual inhibitions were gone and the raunchier the whole evening got, the better we were going to like it.

When I thought about it later, for example, I couldn't remember anyone actually *saying* that we would stand around watching while each of us took a turn with Cherry. This was never put into words, and yet once things got into gear, we all more or less took it for granted that that was how it would go. Normally I would have found that idea a little off-putting. I would have gone along with it, maybe, but I would have at least questioned it a little. You would think it would just be more natural for a group of men to want to make it with the girl in private rather than as part of a group thing. Maybe we all wanted to watch each other with Cherry, and maybe we wanted to *be* watched, but it took the special mood of the eve-

ning for all of this to come into the open and to
be taken so completely for granted by all six of us.

Keegan suddenly increased the pace, and we
were all sort of nodding along in rhythm with him
as he hit his stride and finished. He was no sooner
out than Jimmy Joe was in his place, all hunched
up over Cherry so that he could nibble at her
breasts as he humped away at her. I got a look at
her face. Her eyes were half lidded and her jaw
was slack, and she was drooling a little bit out of
the corner of her mouth. That was about the extent
of her participation in what was going on. She
didn't even move very much, just giving her behind a slight wiggle every once in a while, maybe
to prove to us that she hadn't gone and died somewhere along the way.

Jimmy Joe didn't last very long. After just a few
seconds he started cursing his head off as he
gave a last thrust and came. He was swearing all
the way through, and he went on swearing after he
withdrew, and he walked all the way across the
room still cursing under his breath.

"Hey," Keegan said, pleasantly, "why don't you
put a sock in it, huh? Pipe down."

"Goddamn sonofabitching—"

"Happens to everybody," Keegan said.

"What a time to turn into a rabbit."

"You got excited," I said. The world's foremost authority, Chip Harrison, passing out free advice. "You'll feel easier the second time around."

"Or the third," Keegan said.

Jimmy Joe stopped swearing. Lester was taking his turn, not lying on top of her but standing with his feet on the floor. Maybe all those hours in bus station toilets had him thinking he had to be on his feet to enjoy sex. He had Cherry arranged so that her legs hung over the edge of the bed, and then he picked up her feet and doubled them up with her knees deeply bent, and then he bent over her and got down to brass tacks. It was an interesting position and the rest of us commented on its fine points, like sportsmen checking out a Thoroughbred racehorse.

"He's really getting in that way," Solly noted. "You double 'em up that way, you can just about tickle their tonsils."

Someone else said he preferred to do his work lying down, and the discussion moved along, and Lester turned his head and told us to shut up, managing to do this without missing a beat.

But I noticed something about Cherry. She was starting to get interested in what was happening. Lester had told me this would happen, but I didn't really believe him. It was true, though. There were loads of sweat on her forehead and upper lip now, and between her breasts. She was breathing hard, and her hips were bucking and twitching, and after all the time she had spent just lying there, she was gradually getting into the mood in a big way.

Which meant I was the lucky one, I thought, reaching for the bottle and knocking back another drink. I mean, they were just getting her ready for me. I was the one who was going to have the best time of it.

I guess her excitement had an effect on all of us. The talk gradually died down and stopped completely. The five of us watched in silence, eyes riveted to the two of them on the bed.

Lester finished. He dragged himself off the girl's body and staggered over to the bathroom. Solly took his place and just stood there for a minute, looking down at the girl. I wanted to ask him what the hell he was waiting for, but I didn't break the silence.

He sighed, then put a hand down and touched her between her legs.

She moaned. I guess it was the first sound I could remember hearing her make.

He lifted his hand and looked at it. "Soaking wet," he said to himself. "Dripping, the little mink is dripping. And hot."

Come on, I thought. Come on already.

He entered her slowly, very slowly, and she moaned again, a rippling moan that was unlike any sound I'd ever heard. I was a little worried now that Solly was going to be the lucky one to make her come. It was a pretty silly thing to worry about now that I think back on it, but at the time it seemed very important that I be the one to do this. So I stood there with my hands in fists, wishing that Solly would learn Jimmy Joe's impersonation of a rabbit.

He worked slowly at first, in and out, very slowly, and my whole brain was filled up with the picture of the two of them rolling around on my bed, locked together in this slow thoughtful screw. If there's anything that looks more ridiculous than people screwing, I don't know what it is. I mean, if you stopped to think what you look like when you're doing it, the facial expressions and the position and all, you might not feel as much like going through with it. They looked foolish, but they also looked as though what they were doing was a tremendous amount of fun.

Then bit by bit the tempo picked up, with each of them working at the same pace. She spoke for the first time, begging him to do it harder and faster. She talked nonstop, and she didn't use more than five different words all in all, and three of them were obscene, which is a pretty good average if you spread it over a person's whole vocabulary. She begged him to do it, and he did it, and she wrapped her legs around him and dug her nails into him and really let herself go, kicking and screaming her head off.

Solly gave a cross between a growl and a roar. He pitched forward on her the way Flick had done earlier. But Cherry didn't stop kicking and screaming and wiggling her tail, as if she didn't realize that the record was over. For a few seconds Solly just lay there being tossed around by her hips. Then he grunted and heaved himself up and away from her. She tried to hang on. He unhooked her arms from around his neck and dumped her on the bed.

"She don't know when to quit," he said to no one in particular. I started for her, but he was standing in the way, just shaking his head and saying that she was a crazy little broad who didn't know when to quit.

She was writhing on the bed, making noises like cats fighting under a full moon. "Oh, I almost made it," she said. "Oh, I'll make it this time, somebody, help, please, somebody, I'll make it this time."

Keegan started for her. I grabbed him by the shoulder and spun him around.

"My turn," I said.

"Oh," he lied, "I forgot about you."

"Sure you did."

"Easy, now. If you want to stand arguing, someone'll take your turn. That what you want?"

"You know something, Keegan? I never realized it before, but you know what you are?"

"Lad—"

"You're a son of a bitch, Keegan."

"Easy, now," Keegan said.

"Please," Cherry said. "Please please please please—"

"*Open up in there*," a voice said.

"Please please please—"

"*Open that door.*"

The room went silent again. I had shouldered Keegan aside and was on my way to the girl. Someone grabbed my arm. I shook the hand off.

They kicked the door in. Four cops the size of the Green Bay Packers. One of them went around waving a badge and a gun at everybody, and the other three pulled me off Cherry.

I bit one of them in the leg and hit one of them in the face and kicked one of them in the family jewels. If there had just been the three of them

I think I would have taken them. I really mean it. But the fourth one managed to get behind me and hit me over the head with the butt of his gun.

"Oh, you rats," I heard Cherry howling. "I almost made it. Another minute and I would of made it, you rats. I'll never let you dirty cop rats screw me again. Never, damn you. Oh, I almost made it—"

The gun butt popped me again. The lights went out and so did I.

You know, I can understand how people can become paranoid. It isn't that hard to figure out. When things have been going wrong in one particular way over and over again, it's natural to figure that there's a conspiracy against you.

Take me, for instance. (Take me! I'm yours!) No, seriously. Here I was, for Pete's sake, with just one thing I really wanted to do, and I was being turned at every thwart. I was playing the goddamned Doris Day part in one of those movies where the big question is whether or not Doris can keep her legs together until the end of the film, and the big answer is always yes.

You already know about Francine—remember? to hook your attention? the gun going off—and here I was the last man in line at an orgy and the cops came in just when my number came up.

Why shouldn't I be paranoid? Obviously those cops were just waiting in the hallway for it to be my turn. Obviously someone had switched decks of cards, so that I wound up cutting a deck where every card was the fucking four of clubs. Obviously there was a hole in the wall, or a two-way mirror, and good old Gregor was out there taking pictures and old Haskell was watching and beating off in the name of sociological research, and the Head was laughing, and the basketball coach was saying that a winner never quits and a quitter never wins, and Cherry was taking off her red wig and revealing herself as Aileen, being faithful to Gregor in her peculiar way, and Calvin was saying *Rowrbazzle*, which means *Up your ass* in Siamese, and my parents weren't really dead, they were just trying to escape from their boring mess of a kid.

I couldn't have been unconscious for very long, because the first thing I saw when I opened my eyes was a pair of baggy pants. I watched as the pants were pulled up past my face and onto Flickinger, to whom they belonged. I was lying on the floor next to the bed, and Flickinger was sitting on it, and pulling his pants on.

I stayed where I was. There were conversations going on, but my head was buzzing and I was sort of listening *through* the conversations without hearing them, the way you do when you watch an Italian movie. All I knew was that there were four cops in the room, along with the five guys from the crew. I didn't see or hear Cherry.

I guess I must have realized sort of vaguely that nobody was paying attention to me, and that this was Just As Well. So I was very careful to stay where I was, and I closed my eyes again, and I found out that with my eyes shut my ears worked again, and I listened to what they were saying.

A voice I didn't know, a coppish voice, was saying, "Boy, your ass is grass. You're gone be in jail so long you'll be able to homestead your cell. I just hope you like what you got off of that little girl tonight, because you won't get anything else off anybody else for the next twenty years. Indiana don't care about statutory rape, now. Indiana don't care for that at all."

"She did act like a statue at first," Flick said. "But she was no statue toward the end there. Without you jokers were kicking the door in, she was humping like a camel."

"Now I told you about your rights," the cop said. Or maybe it was another cop. If you've heard one cop, you've heard them all. "And about your rights to an attorney, and how statements made voluntarily may be introduced as evidence in criminal prosecutions against you. You recollect I gave you that warning."

"Cut the shit," Flick said.

"Because you're just digging your grave with your tongue, boy, and I want to make sure you know what you're about."

"Something about raping a statue," Keegan said.

He sounded as unconcerned as Flickinger, and I couldn't understand it. Neither could the cops. The guys were drunk, but it didn't seem possible that they were drunk enough to be this way.

Solly said, "That was no statue, that was my wife."

"Not funny, boy. That young lady was under the age of consent."

"That was no young lady," Lester put in. "That was my statue."

"What's the age of consent here anyway?"

"Eighteen, same as most everywhere else."

"And you mean to say that girl was seventeen?"

"No, sir," the cop said. He sounded very Jack Webbish. "I mean to say she was fifteen."

"Well, I declare," Lester said. "Why, the little liar swore up and down she was thirty-five."

The room rocked with laughter. I didn't laugh, and neither did the cops. They made threatening sounds and talked about going on down to the station house. Jimmy Joe hummed *Dum-Da-Dum-Dum* and got a laugh. Flickinger stood up, stepped over me, and started rasping away in his No More Of This Nonsense voice. He saved it for special occasions, and it was very impressive. He told the cops that they could cut out this shit about warning us of our rights, because the same rights meant that they couldn't kick the door in without a warrant, and since we were in a private room with a closed and locked door, they had no case, and—

"We had a warrant," the cop said.

"Huh?"

"Naming you six men." He read our names. "That's you folks, isn't it?" Flickinger allowed that it was us, all right. I was relieved, for no particular reason, when he read my name as Chip Harrison. When he was going down the list I had the weirdest idea that he was going to read off *Leigh Harvey Harrison,* and that was all I needed.

"And charging you six men with fraud, attempted fraud, soliciting without a license, several counts of trespass and criminal trespass, and miscellaneous violations of the following civic ordinances—" and he read off a batch of numbers.

"Now just a minute," Flick said. He still didn't seem at all worried, and I decided he was crazy. I didn't know what any of those numbers were supposed to mean, but it sounded as though they had enough against us to put us away for hundreds and hundreds of years. And the worst part of all was that this had happened before I could get to Cherry. Whatever jail they put me in, the odds were good that there wouldn't be any women in it, which meant I'd be a male virgin until I was too old to be interested.

I shuddered, then tuned Flick in again. "Where you made your mistake," he was saying, "was that you came down here without you checked it all out with the sheriff. Now if you would of done this we wouldn't have any trouble. Now what you got to do is get on the phone and ring the sheriff and tell him what's happening, and you can let me have a couple of words with him, and we'll have this whole thing straightened out in a minute."

"You and the sheriff are close, is that right?"

"The closest. And there's no hard feelings, and to prove it there'll be something in it for you fellows, too. More or less to make it up to you for your time."

"That's attempting to bribe an arresting officer," the cop said. "Write that down, Ken."

"You'll have to spell it for him," Keegan said, and then there was an *oof* sound, as though someone (like Ken) had hit someone (for instance, Keegan) in the stomach.

"Officer," Flick said, coming down hard on the first syllable, "I think *I* have to spell it out for *you*. The fix is in."

"Is that right?"

"You talk to the sheriff and—"

"I talked to him an hour ago. That's his signature on the bottom of the warrant there, boy."

"Like hell it is."

A long pause. Then Flickinger said, "It says Harold M. Powers. Now who in the precious hell is Harold M-for-Mother Powers?"

The cops all laughed. They really enjoyed themselves. I guess when you're a cop you don't get all that many opportunities to cut loose and laugh, and they made the most of this one. *"Now who in the precious hell,"* one of them started, and they broke up for a while, and another finished, *"is Harold M-for-Mother Powers?"* and they all fell out all over again.

Until finally one of them said, "Why, I'll tell you, boy, if you're so close with him, how come you don't even recognize the sheriff's name?"

"What about Barnett Ramsey?"

"Why, we had an election some six or eight months ago, and old Barney got beat."

"He lost the election," Flickinger said. Heavily.

"After all those years. Yeah, it surprised a whole mess of folks."

"Great bleeding shit," Flickinger said. "Jesus frigging Christ with a tambourine. Holy laminated bifurcated ocellated Mother of Pearl."

"I never heard the like," one cop said softly.

"Sweet shit in a bucket," Flickinger said. "I bribed the wrong man."

Everybody started talking at once. I took a deep breath and said a quick prayer and rolled under the bed.

CHAPTER EIGHT

I DIDN'T REALLY EXPECT TO GET AWAY with it. But they had been doing such a great job of ignoring me that I figured I ought to give them all the encouragement I could. The easier I made it for them, the better.

So I rolled under the bed, and since I was right next to it already, and on the floor, and more or less face down, it wasn't that hard to do. In a sense I suppose *rolled* is the wrong word for it. I sort of crept on my belly like an earthworm. Sideways, though. Earthworms, as you probably know, tend to go back and forth. I don't know how you tell an earthworm's back from his forth. It was never very important to me. I don't even like to go fishing, for Pete's sake. I do know, though, that earthworms are male at one end and female at the other, so you know what they can do.

Lying under that bed, I decided that the police force of the fifth largest city in the state of Indiana could do the same thing earthworms can do, for all I cared. Because it occurred to me that they were not only going to give me the royal shaft, but they were going to give it to me for something I didn't do. In the first place I was only seventeen myself, so what I did to Cherry wasn't statutory rape, and in the second place I hadn't done anything in the first place.

Which seemed to indicate that as soon as I clued them in, they would let me go.

But I didn't think they would. So I stayed under the bed while Flickinger told everybody who would listen that it would take a while to straighten everything out, but that he knew everything would be straightened out, because one thing you couldn't deny was that he and his men represented Dynamic Termite Extermination, Inc., and that DTE was no fly-by-night outfit but a company that had been a leader in its field for twenty-two-count-em-twenty-two years, and that was by God a lot of goddamn years.

(This was the God's honest truth, as a matter of fact. I had trouble believing it myself, but it was. The company didn't ever do a thing that was illegal. If a crew boss ran things on the shady side, they didn't want to know about it. If a crew boss ran things on the up and up, that was fine with DTE. Of course an honest crew boss couldn't possibly clear fifteen cents a month, but that was the way it went. You couldn't call the company crooked just because all its employees were crooked, could you?)

"We'll be out of this in no time," Flick said. "Youse guys just trust me on this without you all lose your heads and get rattled. All right, we gotta go see the Sheriff, that's what we got to do. That's all."

They finished getting dressed, and they talked about things, and they asked the cops if Cherry was really only fifteen, and the cops said she was, and Lester asked one of the cops how often Cherry generally got statutorily raped, and the cop said as often as she possibly could, and Lester asked why anybody would make a fuss over it then, and the cop said it was because it was the sort of thing the city couldn't take lying down, and Lester said that if Cherry could take it lying down, he didn't see why the city couldn't. The cop laughed and said that was sure a good way of putting it. I think this comes under the heading of Fraternizing With The Enemy.

And I kept waiting for somebody to say, "Hey, what happened to the kid we had to hit over the head?"

Or for one of the guys on our side to say, "Say, what the hell happened to Chip?"

Or for somebody, anybody, to sing out, *"Look who's hiding under the bed!"*

But they found other things to say, and the door opened, and they trailed out of it and left it ajar. I don't know to this day where Cherry was during all of this. I didn't see her or hear her, and I didn't hear anybody talk to her, or say anything that gave the impression she was in the room. But I didn't see how she could have been taken anywhere because all of the cops were still in the room, so who would have taken her away? I guess either they sent her home by herself or a matron came for her while I was unconscious. Or else she was what you would call a plant, and the police had sent her over there to begin with so that they could give us all the shaft. (I don't really believe that last one at all. But I'm putting it in to give you an idea of how paranoid a person can get under the right set of circumstances. After all, somewhere out there is my old roommate Haskell, and I want to make sure the book has a certain amount of psychological significance so he won't feel guilty while he reads it and turns the pages with one hand. Hi, Haskell, you hypocritical jerk-off!)

They left the room, as I said before I got off course again. They went out, and I heard them in the hallway, and I got out from under the bed, still waiting for them to wonder what had happened to the kid. I went over to the window and yanked it open. And somebody must have wondered about me, although they were too far away from the room for me to hear them say so, because I heard footsteps racing back up the hall and a voice— Jimmy Joe, God bless him—shout out my name.

I stepped out of the window. It was the first floor, which was the one good thing that had happened that evening. And it was at the back of the motel, away from the parking lot and nowhere near where the other cops had been heading. That was the second good thing that happened that evening. And, because they come in threes, a third good thing happened that evening, which is that I ran like a cat with its tail on fire and got away without being spotted.

Which was very good.

But it could have been better. I mean, even considering the fact that my commissions were all being held for me by the Dynamic Termite Extermination, Inc. office, and that I had been doing my Coke buying and moviegoing out of my own savings for a couple of months, the fact remained that I had over a hundred dollars in my wallet, along with various cards to prove I was me in case I died and they wanted to make sure the body wasn't Judge Crater or Ambrose Bierce. There was also a picture of Aileen that I kind of liked, and that I would miss.

It would have been good if I had been able to bring my wallet. And it would have been even better if I had had something to put my wallet in, because although the night was unseasonably hot, it's never a good idea to rum amok in Indiana's fifth-largest city with no clothing whatsoever on your body.

I've read books where the hero suddenly gets struck naked one way or another. Or he breaks out of jail and has to get something to replace his prison uniform. Or he soaks his clothes swimming to safety and can't wait for them to dry. Or there are these telltale bloodstains telling tales all over the place.

When this happens in books, what the guy usually does is swipe clothing from an untended clothesline. The authors don't generally dwell on it too intently. They just throw something like *Dressing himself with clothes purloined from an un-*

tended clothesline, Stud Boring relentlessly took up the trail of the three pencil sharpeners. Then they plunge right into the action without giving you time to think about it.

In the movies, they're even cooler about it. I saw this done just the night before last, as a matter of fact. This guy broke out of prison, out of a chain gang actually, and one moment you saw him running down the road with his prison clothes all shredded from the brambles and wet from the swamp he went through to throw the dogs off his trail, and then there was another shot of him getting off a bus, wearing a shirt and tie and carrying a leather suitcase. They didn't even cheat by giving you the abandoned clothesline bit. They just came right out and admitted that they didn't know how the hell Stud Boring got those clothes, and that they weren't going to try to fake their way out of it. I suppose you have to admire them for it.

The thing of it is that if you can find a clothesline in the middle of the night, tended or untended, you are better suited to this sort of thing than I was. I don't even think I'd care to look for one in the daytime, because the checking I did showed that (a) people don't leave their clothes hanging out overnight and (b) most of them don't even have clotheslines nowadays. I went zipping through backyards looking for clothes and the whole thing was a large zero. No lines and certainly no clothes. I wouldn't have thought of looking in the first place except that I remembered all those dumb books. You've got to be very suspicious of everything you read.

I think I know what happened. Years ago nobody had clothes dryers, and everybody who washed clothes had to hang them out to dry, and with that many people washing clothes, there would always be a certain number who would forget to take their clothes in for the night, or who wouldn't get around to it because they were baking bread or beating rugs by hand or putting up preserves or watering the horses or any of those good old-time things that people don't do anymore. So in those days it was perfectly open and aboveboard to have Stud Boring steal clothes from a washline. (Open and aboveboard for the writer, I mean. It was still illegal for Stud Boring.)

But nowadays when a writer is trying to get old Stud out of a tight place, the first thing he thinks of is what he read somewhere else. (That's why so many books are the same. The writers all get ideas from each other.) And because they were never running around naked in the middle of the night, they don't know that they'd be better off looking for an abandoned clothes dryer, for Pete's sake, in this modern day and age.

After I figured out that I wasn't going to get clothes off a line, I sat in a dark corner of somebody's garage and tried to think what to do next. I thought about going where the clothes were. Clothes in general. I mean. Not my own clothes, which were all in my room, which was a place I knew better than to go back to. But other clothes, that I could sort of find before they were lost. The first ideas I had all involved breaking into someplace or other. Somebody's house, or some store that sold clothes.

I figured if I broke in anyplace I would get caught, and if I got caught I would be worse off than ever, because in addition to fraud and statutory rape they could also put me in jail for burglary. And while I thought if worst came to worst I could probably get a suspended sentence for the other charges (assuming Flick remembered who to bribe for a change), I could see myself spending a long time in prison for burglary. I also figured anybody breaking into a house or a store stood a very good chance of getting opened up with a shotgun.

Then I thought, but not for long, about Lying In Ambush and crowning somebody with a brick or something heavy, say a traditional Blunt Instrument for example, like a saxophone. Having just been hit on the head myself, I didn't want to do the same to a stranger. Besides that, you may remember that I'm not even coordinated enough to pace the Upper Valley basketball team to a regional title, and that I get nauseous just thinking about violence for any length of time. I was violent enough with the three cops, but that's something else. I mean, I had something to fight for.

Then I tripped over a muddy shoe.

To give you an idea how brilliant I was, I looked at what I tripped over and said to myself, Oh, it's a shoe, and put it out of the way so I wouldn't trip over it again. And I must have sat around scheming for another five minutes before I remembered that shoes were things you wear on your feet, and that I wasn't wearing any at the moment, and that, therefore, a muddy shoe was better than no shoe at all, and I ought to follow the old proverb that starts out *If the shoe fits.*

Here's another proverb. *If the shoe doesn't exactly fit, wear it anyway, because shoes are almost as hard to come by as clotheslines.*

These shoes were a little loose, and down at the heels, and thin in the soles, and one of the laces had been broken and tied together again. If they'd been in better shape, the owner wouldn't have used them for gardening and I wouldn't have tripped over them, so I didn't really have any right to complain.

I didn't have time to complain, either. Because I figured out that some people had special shoes that they used for gardening or painting or any kind of yard work, and others had special pants and shirts, and that if I looked in enough garages I could probably put together a wardrobe that would get me a lot of curious glances, I'll admit, but that would, all things considered, get me less attention than my present costume of shoes and nothing else.

Some people lock their garages, but most of them don't. Most people don't have anything wearable in their garages, but some of them do. And I wasn't fussy about fit or looks or style, and garages are fairly easy to get in and out of without disturbing anybody, and to make a long story short (or at least as short as possible, at this stage of the game) I wound up wearing the muddy shoes and a pair of paint-blotched dungarees and a red-and-black plaid hunter's jacket and a little peaked gardener's cap.

And in the same garage where I found the hunter's jacket I found something else, and while it didn't take the nose of a bloodhound to ferret it out (or the nose of a ferret to bloodhound it out), I'm going to come right out and say that it was brilliant of me to take it along. Look, I've told you about all of the idiot things, so I might as well take whatever credit I can get.

It was a fishing rod. The way I was dressed, there were only two things on earth I could be— a criminal on the run or a lunatic fisherman. So I took the fishing rod and transformed myself from a Threat To Society to an All-American Boy, and I walked right through the dippy town without a bit of trouble.

If this was a movie, the thing to do now would be to cut straight on through fo September. Not for the sake of cheating, the way they do when they refuse to tell you how Stud Boring got dressed again, but just because nothing very interesting happened during the next two months. And if we just cut to two months later and fifteen hundred miles east of there, you wouldn't miss much.

But if you're like me you always want to know about things like that, like what happened during the two months it took me to get from the fifth largest city in Indiana to where I was in September, which is also where I am now. If I like a book and get interested, I want to know everything.

When it comes to novels, I like the old-fashioned approach where they tell you what happened to the characters after the book ended. You know, the plot's all tied up and the story is all used up and done with, and then there's a last chapter where the author explains that Mary and Harold got married and had three children, two boys and a girl, and Harold lived to be sixty-seven when a stroke got him, and Mary survived him by twenty years and never remarried, and George went back together with his wife but they broke up again after three years, and George went to California and has never been heard from since, and his wife died of pleurisy the year after he left. I like to feel that the people are so real that they go on doing things even when the book is done with them, and sometimes I'll make up my own epilogue for a book in my head if the author didn't write one himself. It's called an epilogue when you do this.

Anyway, ever since I started writing this, in fact ever since Mr. Burger said I really ought to write it, I decided I would just act as though the person reading it was more or less like myself. With a similar way of looking at things and so on. So whenever I have to decide whether to put something in or not, I ask myself whether or not I would want to read it. That's why I put in all that crap about the termite racket, for example.

What I did for the rest of July and all of August and the first week of September was farm work, for the most part. I headed east when I left town and didn't stop walking and hitchhiking until I was in Ohio. I didn't think the police would bother sending out an alarm for me, since I wasn't exactly Public Enemy Number One. I mean I wasn't the most sought-after criminal since Arlo Guthrie dumped the garbage in Stockbridge, Mass. I was breathing fairly easy as soon as I got out of the county, but I still thought it would be good to get across the state line without taking any chances.

I kept getting lifts for a couple of miles at a time because this particular highway wasn't one that anybody would take for any great distance. But on a bigger road I would have stood out like acne with my clothes and my fishing rod. On this road people either assumed I was going to a particular fishing spot or when they asked I would just say *Down the road a piece* and they figured I was keeping the spot a secret. Fishermen do crazy things like that all the time. Then I would just sit in the car until they let me out because they were turning off.

Eventually, though, I got sick of having to talk about fishing with people who all knew more about it than I did. And I got sick of carrying the pole. So I left it on a bridge over a little creek that I happened to walk over between rides. I figured whoever found it would be able to get some use out of it right away.

Then, since I didn't have the pole, people assumed I was a drifter, which was what I was, actually. And one man said, "Bet you're looking to get work picking. Cherries is gone but early peaches is coming in, and won't be a week and they be picking summer apples, the weather the way she be."

I hadn't even thought about it. I wasn't in shape to think any further than the Ohio line, to tell the truth. But farm work sounded as good as anything else I could think of, and it turned out to be just right, considering the circumstances.

You didn't need a car or a suit or a degree or any experience whatsoever. You could walk in off the road wearing paint-smeared dungarees and muddy shoes and a hunting jacket and not get looked at twice. If they had berries or melons that needed picking, or peaches or apples or sweet corn or tomatoes, they didn't care where you went to school or who your father was or if you had a Social Security card. All they cared was if you wanted to get out in the field and pick the stuff.

Of course they didn't pay much, either. They

really couldn't. Look, a pint of blueberries, say, will cost you maybe half a dollar at the supermarket, right? Suppose the farmer who grew it got half of that, which he never does, I don't think, unless he sells it himself or something. But anyway, say he gets a quarter a pint. Now if you ever picked blueberries you know that it takes forever to fill a pint container with the stupid little things. You could get the whole quarter for picking those berries and it wouldn't be exactly the highest wages in history, and that would mean the farmer was giving the berries away for nothing.

But even with the pay low, and even with being on your feet all day, and getting up early in the morning and working twelve or fourteen hours at a stretch, even with all of that, there were good things about it. Even with the backache you got from picking stuff that grew on the ground, or the bruises you got from falling off ladders while picking stuff that grows on trees, it was still a good way to cover two months and fifteen hundred miles.

For one thing, you could really eat as though food was free, because it just about was. You were expected to eat all you wanted of whatever you were picking while you picked it. (This was more of a thrill when what you were picking was red raspberries than when it happened to be summer cooking apples.) You also got three meals a day. Breakfast was three or four eggs fresh from the hen and home-baked bread and jam. All the fruits and vegetables were fresh at lunch and dinner, and they kept passing huge oval bowls full of different things around the table.

I had never eaten like that in my life. Not to say anything against my mother, but she wasn't the world's greatest cook. I suppose when you can function as a confidence woman for twenty years without ever getting caught, you can also let other people do the cooking for you. Still, I ate better at home than I did at any of the camps or schools I went to, and from the last school I had gone more or less directly to Aileen's instant coffee and nondairy creamer and TV dinners, moving on to third-rate restaurant food in Illinois and Indiana towns. I had gotten so I never cared much about food, probably because I didn't really know what good food tasted like. I always thought I hated vegetables, for instance, because the ones I ate always came out of cans or plastic bags and then sat on the stove for a couple of months.

Besides the food, the life was just generally healthy. They usually let you sleep in the barn, except a couple of times in large apple orchards in New York State, where there were just more pickers than there was floor space. Even then they took care of us, though, with straw mattresses to sleep on and sheets of canvas to tie to the trees and sleep under, not just because it might rain but so that apples wouldn't drop on top of you.

What I mostly picked was apples. Supposedly you could make better money working vegetable farms, but I really hated the stooping, and I never got used to the feel of the sun on the back of my neck. An apple orchard is cool on hot days and had a great smell to it and you work standing up. Of course you have to expect to fall off the ladder once in a while. They say that anybody who doesn't fall now and then isn't picking fast enough. I won't say that you get used to falling off ladders, or that you grow to look forward to it, but in all the time I picked apples, I never got more than a bruise or saw anybody do worse than sprain a wrist. You learn how to fall after the first couple of times, and it sort of struck me, during one of the moments of philosophical reflection that you get plenty of in an apple orchard, that anybody who lived the kind of life I did really ought to learn how to fall.

The average apple knocker is in his twenties and grew up in the country and quit school young and keeps his mouth shut and likes to get in a fight when he's had a couple of drinks. The average apple knocker is a guy, and so is the unaverage apple knocker. There were no girls up in those trees or out in those barns or under those canvas ceilings.

There was always the farmer's daughter, but she was a long ways away from what she was like in the jokes. Generally she was home on vacation from college, and she would no sooner go off with a picker than she'd pick her nose in church. Her main object was to get pinned to a fraternity boy and live in big city where he could get rich sitting at a desk.

Now and then I would manage to meet a girl. Actually a picker could make out pretty well if he happened to be good at it. In any given area there would be certain taverns and bowling alleys that all the pickers would congregate at when they were in the neighborhood. The taverns generally had either a combo or a jukebox primed with country music. The bowling alleys had balls and pins. The pickers would holler and stomp and get drunk and fight, and occasionally someone would get cut up. You wouldn't believe how casual some of these guys would be about this. A guy might have a scar from his neck to his navel, and if you asked about it he would say, "Oh, my buddy over

there cut me a touch when we were drinking."
And they would still be buddies and joke about
it, and eventually they would have another fight
and the knives would come out again.

Girls would come to the taverns, and especially
to the bowling alleys—I guess it was more respect-
able for a girl to go to a bowling alley, although
you never saw any of them actually go so far as
to bowl. And the girls who came to these places
were there to get picked up by the pickers, and
they knew that pickers were only interested in
One Thing, and it wasn't discussions of the Great
Books Of The Western World. So any girl who
went with a picker was just about putting it in
writing that she was willing to put out. That saved
a lot of time and wasted effort on both sides, and
in a business where you were never in one place
very long, it made things simpler all around.

The thing was that you had to be a certain type
of person to make out under those conditions. The
makeout type, you might say. And it was a type
that I obviously wasn't. The guys who were best
as it were basically pretty stupid guys who could
carry on a conversation all night long without saying anything worth hearing. But they never had
to stop and think about anything. Instead they had
this loose easy style that I guess made it easy for

a girl to relax or something. Whatever it was, I just didn't have it. Whenever I tried to make out at taverns, I would get involved in a conversation with a girl, and she would seem interested, and then she would say she had to go to the ladies' room. And I'd see her five minutes later going home with some other picker.

The girls I dated were girls you could talk to and girls you could have a pleasant evening with. One of them was on vacation from Fredonia State Teachers College, where she was having an awful time with required science courses: she just couldn't seem to get the hang of what they were all about. Another one wanted to talk about liberal religious movements. She didn't believe in God anymore but she was afraid she wouldn't have anything to do on Sunday mornings. She sure won't want to spend them in bed unless she changes a lot, because by the time I got rid of her I needed treatment for frostbite.

There were girls I didn't get to first base with, and there were girls I did get to first base with. And some I got to second base with, and one or two who let me get all the way to third. More than one or two, maybe. But one way or another they all turned in superb clutch pitching, and no matter how many hits I got, the inning would end in a scoreless tie, with my men stranded all over the bases.

I wanted to take my bat and balls and go home.

The last apples I picked were in a small Early MacIntosh orchard in Dutchess County, New York. That's about sixty or seventy miles from New York City. When we finished picking those trees, I all of a sudden knew that I didn't want to pick another apple for a very long time, or anything else. The high season was just coming on, and it was the one time of the year when a fruit picker can actually make decent money, but I was sick of it and ready for something else. I was just done and that was all.

I had around thirty dollars and two changes of clothes including one pair of heavy boots and a pair of regular shoes. I also had a whole load of money coming to me from the termite sales. I was dumb enough to send them a couple of wires asking them to send me the dough. Of course I never heard from them.

One of two things happened: (a) Flickinger managed to bribe his way out of the mess, in which case he certainly wouldn't tell the office what had happened, so they would treat me like any deserter, or (b) they were all rotting in jail, and nobody ever so much as turned those signed orders in, and there was no money coming to me.

Either way, I had thirty dollars. Which means I had made a clear profit of a dollar a month since I left Upper Valley. I had a lot of vocational experience, none of which would get me a job with Opportunity For Advancement. And my cherry, like the winter apples, was still on the tree.

That's how I spent the summer. The more I think of it, the more I figure the movies have the right idea. Start with a long shot of a kid in muddy shoes and a hunter's jacket on a dusty Indiana road, and cut to a shot of the same kid finishing a hard day's work as a wiper in a car wash in Upstate New York. In a town which I won't name, because I'm still here now, writing this, and may be here forever.

It was in this very town that I met Francine.

Remember Francine?

To tell you the absolute truth, I'm having a little trouble remembering her myself. Good old Burger told me it was always a good idea to start off with something dramatic to hook the reader, and then go back and fill in the background and work up to it, but I have a feeling that would have been a better idea if I were someone who knew something about writing a book. If I were starting over again, I would just start at the beginning and go straight through to the end and the hell with hooking your attention and riveting your eye to the page. Either you're with me or you're not. But in case you forgot about Francine, and how things were going when I broke off to start backing and filling, it went like this:

And paused, because it seemed tnat a herd of elephants was stampeding up the staircase and down the hall, and voices were shouting, and Francine was roaring at me, begging me to do it, to stick it in, and I lay there, paralyzed, and the door to my room exploded inward, and a man the size of a mountain charged inside. He had a hand the size of a leg of lamb, and in that hand he had a gun the size of a cannon.

"You son of a bitch!" he bellowed.

And pointed the gun at me, and pulled the trigger.

CHAPTER NINE

THE GUN JAMMED.

CHAPTER TEN

WELL, WHAT DID YOU EXPECT?

Blood?

Look, a guy stuck a gun in my face and pulled the trigger. Now if the gun didn't jam then he would have blown my head off and you would be reading something else because I wouldn't be around to write this.

I mean, I can just hear you clucking like a chicken and saying, "Now how in the hell is he going to get out of this one?" And then on the last page it said *The gun jammed* and you said, "Oh, shit, *the gun jammed,* what a cornball way to save him."

I didn't *plan* it that way, for Pete's sake. If you want to know something, it took me a full day to write the last chapter. One stupid page with three stupid words on it and it took me all day to write it because I couldn't figure out how to tell you that the gun jammed. And finally it came to me that there was only one way. *The gun jammed.* Period, end of chapter.

I'll tell you something. I was going to make something up instead of having the gun jam. You know, to lie to you and figure out something more convincing and satisfying than a jammed gun. (I already put two things in this book that aren't true. They're out-and-out lies, actually. They're both in the second chapter. If you think you know what they are, write to me. I'd be interested to see if you get it right.)

But I couldn't think of a lie. Either I'm dictating this from the grave or the gun jammed. Well, the gun jammed and that's all there is to it, and come to think of it, I don't know why in the hell I'm apologizing, because what it amounts to is I'm apologizing for being *alive*, and that doesn't make any sense.

CHAPTER ELEVEN

WHEN HE SAW THAT THE GUN WAS JAMMED, he tried wiggling the trigger with his finger. It wouldn't come back into position. I suppose that was the logical time to pick up a chair and brain him with it, while he was standing there playing with the gun and swearing at it, but I don't have those kind of reflexes. I just sat there on the bed with one hand on my knee and the other on the best part of Francine and waited for him to get the gun fixed and shoot me all over again.

Then he looked at me and said, "You're not Pivnick." His voice was very stern, as if he was *accusing* me of not being Pivnick. As though Pivnick was something everybody should be, like clean or loyal or trustworthy.

"No," I said, "I'm not."

"I was sure it was Pivnick. I would have sworn up and down it was Pivnick." He frowned. Then he looked up again and turned his eyes on Francine.

"You," he said. "You're not Marcia."

She didn't say anything. "No," I said, for her. "She's not Marcia. She's Francine."

"No wonder you're not Pivnick." He frowned again, deep in conversation, and then nodded his head emphatically. "Of course," he said. "Of course. I see it all now. That's why you're not Pivnick."

"It's the main reason."

"Then where is my wife?"

"Huh?"

"My wife," he snapped. "Marcia. My wife."

"Oh, Marcia," I said. "Well, it's obvious, isn't it?"

"Tell me."

"She must be with Pivnick."

"Ha," he said, triumphantly. "I thought so! I always thought so. But where?" He lowered his head and paced, then raised it and snapped.

"There is another apartment in this building?"

"No. Just the barbershop downstairs."

"This is One-eighteen South Main Street?"

"Yes."

"Damn it to hell," he said. "I was told I would find them at One-eighteen South Main Street. I was told that it was Pivnick. But I was certain. And I was definitely told that it was my wife. They told me I would find her at One-eighteen South Main Street in Rhinebeck."

"This isn't Rhinebeck."

"*What?*"

"This isn't Rhinebeck," I told him. And I told him the name of the town.

"Damn it to hell," he said. "I knew I had made a mistake as soon as I saw it wasn't Pivnick. But what a mistake! What an extraordinary mistake! Marcia will never believe this!"

He was glowing and bubbling. Then his face went suddenly somber, as if he just had a power failure. "But I could have killed you," he said. "An innocent man. I could have shot you down in hot blood. And you were not even Pivnick."

"Not for a moment."

"My God," he said. He looked at the gun in his hand and shuddered. Then he jammed it into his pocket, bowed halfway to the floor, apologized to both of us for the interruption, and headed for what was left of my door. Very little was. He took two steps and the gun went off in his pocket. He lost two toes on his right foot, and it was hell getting the bleeding stopped. I thought sure the cops would come and let him go and arrest me for picking apples out of season. The cops didn't come.

"Bostonians," he said, dully, looking at his feet.

"Marcia and Pivnick?"

"The shoes! One-hundred-and-ten-dollar Bostonians!" He glared at them. "And only seven years old. The salesman swore they would last a lifetime. Bostonians!"

I considered pointing out that one of them was still in perfectly good shape, as were eight of his toes. But I kept this to myself.

Francine ripped up a pillowcase to make bandages. I fixed him up and told him he ought to go to a hospital. He said he had to go to Rhinebeck. I don't know if he ever found Pivnick or not, but if I were Marcia I would be very goddamned careful from now on.

Once we were rid of Marcia's husband, Francine remembered that she didn't have any clothes on. It was really pretty funny. Before the jerk kicked the door in, it was easy enough for her to pretend that she didn't know what was happening, or that we were just necking a little, or whatever she wanted to pretend. And while he was there waving the gun in the air and talking about Pivnick, we both had too much to worry about to think about being naked. But then he went out and closed my broken door behind him, and there we were. I turned to look at Francine, and she pulled a bedsheet over her really sensational body and tried to look everywhere but at me.

I got onto the bed and scurried over next to her.

"My," she said, "I really have to be getting home now, Chip."

"Oh, it's real early, Francine."

"What a strange man! I thought he was going to shoot you or something."

"Well, he tried."

She talked about him, the sort of brainless talk Francine was good at, and meanwhile I got a hand under the sheet and kept putting it on Francine, and she kept moving it off without missing a beat.

Then she said, "I wish you would cover yourself up, Chip."

"Huh?"

"You don't have any clothes on."

"It's a warm night."

"Be nice, Chip."

"Huh?"

She chewed her lip. "I shouldn't even be here.

I don't know what got into me." Nothing, I thought. "But I guess I just got carried away because of the things you said and how sweet a boy you are. You're very sweet, Chip."

I went to kiss her, but she got her mouth out of the way very skillfully. "Be nice," she said.

"Nice? I thought we would sort of get back to what we were doing."

"I don't know what you mean by that."

"Before he walked through the door."

"I don't know what—"

"Well, just for the record, Francine, we were about to make love."

"Really, Chip, I don't—"

"I mean I was lying on top of you, for Christ's sake, and you were telling me to shove it in all the way to your neck. I mean let's not pretend we don't know our names, for Pete's sake. I mean that's what we were doing before we were so rudely interrupted, and I don't see why all of a sudden we have to pretend that we just met each other at a church picnic."

She was staring at me.

"I mean it seems pretty silly," I said.

She turned away from me. "You're a very crude boy," she said.

"A minute ago I was very sweet."

"I thought you were, but obviously I was mistaken. I shouldn't even be here."

"Well, give me a minute and I'll cut the ropes."

"What?"

"The ropes that are tying you down so you can't escape my evil clutches. I'll cut you loose and you can hurry home."

"Chip—"

"What?"

She sighed a couple of times. Her eyes stole a look at me, moving over my body to the part of me she wanted me to pull a sheet over. She withdrew them, but they came back again of their own accord.

She said, "If you would just be a gentleman, and if you would tell me the things you said before, you know, about thinking I'm really pretty and that you like me as a person and you respect me, then everything could be the way it was before."

I made her say it again. And she said it again in just about the same words.

"That's a great idea," I said. "Say, do you suppose we should put our clothes on first so that we can start over from the beginning?"

"That would be best, Chip."

"That sure is a great idea," I said.

"I'm glad you—Chip, *what* are you *doing*?"

"What does it look like I'm doing?"

"Chip, now *stop* that!"

"It's my thing," I said, "If I want to play with it, I've got every right in the world."

"If you think I'm going to sit here and watch you, you're out of your mind!"

"Would you like to do it for me?"

"Chip, I don't know what's the matter with you."

"Go home."

"But I thought—"

"Go home."

"Chip?"

"Go home."

When she went home, I stopped playing with myself. I was only doing it to annoy her. I mean, I wouldn't want you thinking that I got any kick out of it, at least in a sexual sense. But it sure got old Francine's teeth on edge, and that was the general idea.

After she left I sat around for a while. I got dressed again and had a look at the door. If the barber saw it he was going to have a fit and if he didn't see it I didn't want him cutting my hair, because he would be likely to lop off an ear. I mean it was smashed beyond recognition. You couldn't make it look like a door again. The only way to hide it was to hang a picture over it, and I didn't know where to get one at that hour.

What I did was take the door right off its hinges and carry the whole mess downstairs. I put all the pieces back with the garbage from the drugstore two doors down. The next time Mr. Bruno asked for the rent, I asked him when he was going to bring my door back.

"Door? What door? I never tooka your door."

"Then where did it go?"

"Jeez," he said, and added something in Italian. The next day two of his sons came and hung a new door for me. The next time I saw old Bruno he said he was sorry they had taken the door off without telling me, but it needed painting. I got so I had trouble knowing whether that guy kicked my door in or not.

But all this is off the subject. I guess I'm trying to duck the obvious question, which is was I losing my mind or what?

Because Francine would have let me do it. She just about came right out and said she would let me do it if only I would play up to her the way she wanted. She spelled it out for me, just about, and I wasn't so dumb that I didn't get the message, and what did I do? I sent her home, for Pete's sake. I sat there, pulling my pud like a total dip and told her to take her whatchamacallit and go home, and kept telling her until she went.

I sat around for hours trying to figure it out. And the best I could come up with was that I had just been trying to get laid for so long that finally something snapped inside me and I just wasn't going to go through all that goddamn nonsense again. If you stop to think, ever since I left Upper Valley I had been planning on working hard and applying myself and being straightforward and open and honest and sensible, all in a heroic All-American effort to Get Ahead. And time after time I wound up being dishonest and sneaky and con-niving, and floated around aimlessly and didn't save money and wasn't getting ahead, and all be-cause the only thing I really gave a damn about was getting laid. And it might have made sense if I was making out like a maniac, but I wasn't getting anyplace at all, and the whole thing just wasn't worth the trouble.

And Francine wasn't worth the trouble, for Pete's sake. No matter how nice her body was, there was too thick a layer of stupidity and selfishness hovering over it. And no matter what terrific secrets she had hidden between her legs, they just couldn't be worth all the games and crap you had to go through to get to her.

I just wasn't interested.

You may have trouble believing it. I don't blame you for a minute. This is I, Chip Harrison, talking, after all, and to tell you the truth, I didn't believe it all myself. But it was true.

I went outside and walked around until I found a place to have a cup of coffee. I just walked right in and sat down at the counter without giving the place the usual carefully casual are-there-any-girls-here glance. I didn't even care. I sat at the counter, and the waitress who always served me came over and gave me the usual big phony smile and leaned forward to give me the usual cheap thrill, and I talked to her the same way I always did but without even pausing to think for a moment that I would like to bang her. I drank my coffee and ordered another cup. I told myself I might be a virgin for the rest of my life, and if that was the way it was going to be, I would just have to learn to live with it, because no matter how great Doing It felt (and I don't suppose it would really feel a whole hell of a lot different from some of the things I had done with Aileen, as far as that goes), it still couldn't be worth making a horse's ass of yourself or building your whole life around. It just wasn't worth it.

I was having a third cup of coffee, which I don't usually do, but this wasn't my usual kind of evening, either. A voice said, "Say, is anybody sitting here?"

I turned around. It was a girl about my age, with long brown hair and very wide brown eyes. She was wearing a pair of those granny glasses and if anything they made her eyes look bigger.

"No one at all," I said.

"What I meant was, do you feel like company or are you involved with your own private thoughts?"

"Company's fine."

"Are you sure? I don't want to come on heavy or anything."

"I'm sure. I ran·out of thoughts, anyway."

She parked herself on the stool next to mine. The waitress came over and showed off her breasts. The girl ordered coffee, and I said I didn't want anything, thanks just the same. The waitress gave me one of those tentative dirty looks, as though she didn't know whether to take that the wrong way or not. She brought the girl's coffee and went away.

"I think I've seen you around," the girl said.

"I've been around."

"Are you living in town?"

"For the time being. Just passing through, actually."

"I've been living here for years, but I'm on my way out now. I'm going to college tomorrow morning."

"Oh."

She stirred her coffee. "My first year. I guess I must be a little nervous about it because I couldn't sleep. I had to get out of the house. I didn't think I was nervous but I must be."

"Maybe you're just excited. That can happen."

"I guess so. Do you go to school now or did you finish?"

"I sort of dropped out."

"That's groovy. I guess I'll probably drop out. Most of the kids I know who went already, the more interesting ones, all dropped out after a year or two. But I wanted to see what it was like first."

"That's probably a good idea."

"That's what I figured." She drummed the countertop with her fingers. Her fingernails were chewed ragged and the backs of her hands were brown from the sun. "I'm a Capricorn. Open to new ideas. I believe in that, I think, but I don't know much about it. Astrology, I mean. What are you?"

"Oh. Virgo."

"My name's Hallie."

"Mine's Chip."

"That's very together. I like that." She sipped her coffee and made a face.

"It's pretty bad coffee," I said.

"The worst. But everybody's closed at this hour. Do you work or what?"

"Over at the car wash. They wash and I dry."

"That sounds fair enough."

"I don't love it, but it's a job."

"I think that's where I may have seen you. And you know, walking around."

I looked at her again. "I've seen you, too. I think. With a sort of stocky guy? With shoulders?"

"My brother."

"Oh."

"He's in the Service. The Infantry."

"Oh."

"He enlisted to get it over with and now he's sorry. He hates it."

"I can imagine."

"He thought it would get better after basic training, but he says it's the same shuck all around, and now he thinks they're going to send him overseas."

"Rough."

"You know it."

I looked at her again. She was damned attractive, although it was the kind of good-lookingness that you didn't notice right off. It didn't wave and shout at you, but after you saw it a few times you began to appreciate it. She looked very clean and cool and casual, and she talked with her whole face. I mean, she didn't keep throwing smiles and winks at you and do things with her eyebrows, nothing like that. But the expression on her face always went along with what she was saying. A lot of the time a person's mouth will go off in one direction while their mind is somewhere else.

We didn't talk about anything very important. I told her about some of the apple knockers I had met, and she talked about spending summers on her uncle's farm when she was a kid. I hadn't really talked to a girl this way in I don't know how long. I used to talk to Aileen in Chicago, but that was all screwed up by the fact that I was all hung up on her sexually. With Hallie, sex didn't have anything to do with it. Not that she wouldn't have appealed to me, but that I had gone through some real changes and I wasn't the same horny kid I had been a couple of hours ago.

She had a second cup of the terrible coffee, and I kept her company and had a fourth. When she finished hers I said I thought I would probably go for a walk, and she said maybe some fresh air would do her good, help her get to sleep. We each paid for our own coffee and went outside together.

We walked two or three blocks without talking. But it was an easy silence, not one of those uncomfortable ones where you try to think of something to say and keep running different sentences through your mind. It was completely relaxed. I didn't even get lost in my own thoughts. I just walked along, hardly thinking of anything.

Then she said, "Chip?" I looked at her and for a second her eyes seemed so deep that I could see for miles into them. Then she lowered them and shifted her weight from one foot to the other.

She said, "I live at home with my folks."

"I know."

"We could go to your place."

"If you're tired of walking, sure."

"I mean if you wanted to ball or anything. Not to come on strong, but like I have to go to college tomorrow so there's no time to let things just happen. I think they would happen because I sort of dig you and everything, and even our signs are compatible, Virgo and Capricorn, or at least I think they are, but I don't really know much about it. Astrology."

"Neither do I."

"So if you don't want to, just say so." Her teeth attacked her lower lip. "Whatever you say."

"I live upstairs of Bruno's Barbershop. On the next block."

"I know where it is."

"There's no door to my room. It got broken and I had to take it off, but there's nobody else in the place at night so it doesn't matter if there's a door or not."

"How did the door get broken?"

"A guy kicked it in. If you don't mind about there not being a door—"

"Well, it wouldn't matter if we're the only ones in the building, would it?"

"No."

"So," she said.

I took hold of her hand. It felt much smaller in mine than you would have expected. We walked to the corner, turned, went to my place, and climbed the stairs. I put a light on and apologized for the mess. She said it didn't matter. She said it looked romantic, with the slanting roof and the exposed rafters. "Like a garret," she said. "You'll be a great but unknown artist dying of tuberculosis and I'll be your mistress and model, and you'll get drunk and cough and spit blood and beat me."

I kissed her. She kissed in the same fresh open way she talked, holding nothing back. We stood there kissing for a long time.

Then she took her sweatshirt off and turned around so that I could unhook her bra for her. She kicked off her sandals and stepped out of her dungarees and threw all her clothes in the corner. She stood watching eagerly as I got my clothes off and tossed them after hers. She put out her hand and touched me, and we floated down onto the bed like falling leaves.

"Oh, wow," she said. She burrowed close to me, her head tucked under my arm. "That was—"

"Uh-huh."

"Like unbelievable."

"Yeah."

"It's never been this good for me before." She rolled over on her back and folded her hands together just below her breasts. I looked at her. She said, "I wish they were bigger."

"They're beautiful."

"Tiny."

"So?"

"So I can never be an actress in Italian movies."

"I can't play basketball."

"Huh?"

"Nothing important."

She sat up, looked down at me. "That's the cutest thing," she said.

"I'm sort of attached to it."

"So am I, but in another way. It's so beautiful. Do you think it would get all embarrassed if I gave it a kiss?"

"There's only one way to find out."

She curled into a ball and nestled her head in my lap. Her hair was clean and silky all over my legs.

"Close your eyes," she said.

I closed them, but then I cheated and opened them again. It was so beautiful to watch her. She had her eyes shut and her face glowed with contentment. She looked like a baby nursing.

She stopped to say, "What a funny taste!"

"That's you."

"It is? I guess it must be. Funny."

She came up for air again to say, "It must like me. Look how big it got."

"Uh-huh."

"I really groove on sucking you. Is that terribly perverted of me?"

"Only of you don't do anything else."

"What else should I do?"

I stretched her out on her back and showed her.

Later on she was dozing lightly. I put my hand on her arm and her eyes opened.

"I don't want to scare you or anything, Hallie, but did I hurt you before?"

"I don't think so. Why?"

"Well, look." I pointed to the stain. "That must have come from one of us, and I wouldn't say anything, but if I *did* hurt you or anything—"

"Oh," she said.

"I just thought—"

"I guess I bled a little. I didn't realize."

"Is that common? I mean, oh, do you usually?"

She turned away. "Well, see—"

"What?"

"I should have told you, I guess. But we had such a good thing going and I didn't want anything to get in the way." Her eyes met mine. "I'm a virgin. I mean I was. Until just now. Chip? What's so funny?"

"Nothing."

"Then why are you laughing?"

"It's not important." I put my hands on her. "Look, when do you have to get up in the morning? What I'm getting at is how much longer can you stay?"

"I should have been asleep hours ago."

"Oh."

"But there's time, Chip, if that's what you meant. In fact, you don't even have to hurry. There's plenty of time, actually."

EPILOGUE

I ALREADY TOLD YOU THAT I LIKE epilogues, and knowing what happened to the characters after the story ended. Actually there isn't too much I can put in this particular epilogue because not that much time has passed since then. And the only character I know what happened to is me, and I'm still in the same room over the same barbershop. I've got a new door, but other-wise things are about the same.

But I figured this is probably the only book I'll ever write, so when else am I ever going to get a chance to write an epilogue?

Hallie went home, and the next morning she left for college. She said she would drop a card with her address on it, and if I was ever in Wisconsin I could look her up. I haven't gotten the card yet.

Mr. Bruno replaced my door. I guess I already told you about that, though. And he didn't exactly ask about the bullet hole in his ceiling. "You a gooda boy," he said at one point, as if willing himself to believe it. "You donta shoot anybody, and anybody donta shoota you." He seemed vaguely frightened of me after that.

The car wash closed for the winter. This happened almost immediately, and when they told me, I had the crazy feeling that they were closing the car wash because Hallie had gone to college. In a way it was sort of like that. More people get their cars washed in the summer than in the winter anyway, and this is especially true in this particular city, where there are all sorts of people up for the summer from New York City. So when the summer is over and college kids go back to school and summer people go back to the city, there's not enough business to support the car wash. I was out of a job, but since it wasn't one with an Outstanding Opportunity For Advancement, I wasn't what you might call shattered.

Then I happened to get to talking with Mr. Burger. I was lying around my room, reading a book and wondering where I would go next, and what would I do when I got there, when old Bruno came tearing up the stairs to tell me that one of his customers had a flat tire. "You change it, he give-a you money," he said.

I changed it and he gave-a me a dollar. The car was a Lincoln Continental Mark III. Not that it's any more work changing the tire on an expensive car, but if it had been, say, a beat-up '51 Ford, then I might not have been exactly staggered by getting a lousy dollar for changing it. I still don't think I would have been overwhelmed, though.

"Gee," I said, "thanks very much. Now I can go get a hamburger and maybe some french fries. Man, I can hardly wait."

"Sounds as though you haven't eaten in a long time," Mr. Burger said.

He missed the point, but I went along with it. "I'm out of work," I said, "but through no fault of my own. The position was temporary and the work seasonal."

"The car wash," he said, snapping his fingers. "You were the kid who wiped the windows on the passenger's side."

"I remember your car now. You brought it in every Friday night."

"As soon as I got up from the city. That's

right." He offered me a cigarette. I took it even though I don't smoke, and told him that if it was all right with him I would save it and smoke it later, after my meal. He gave me a funny look, then said sure, he didn't care, and lit his own cigarette. "So you're out of work," he said. "Tough break, all right. I wish I could help you out, but I'm afraid I'm not in the car wash business myself."

"What business are you in?"

"Publishing."

"What type?"

"Books," he said warily. "What makes you ask?"

"No reason."

"Because I haven't got anything for a person without experience."

"Oh, I've got experience," I said. "I've got more experience than you would believe, even if it won't do me any good. I've done more things in the past nine or ten months—"

"I can imagine. When I was your age—" He shook his head. "What did I give you, a buck? Why don't you hang on to it and I'll buy you that hamburger you were drooling over and we'll talk."

"About what?"

"I don't know. Maybe we can do each other some good."

So Mr. Burger worked up a contract for my book and gave me money for living expenses and bought me a typewriter and got me a beautiful blond secretary.

Not really.

What he did, really, was listen to me, talk about where I'd been and what I'd done, and nod every now and then, and smoke a lot of cigarettes, and wonder why I wouldn't smoke one but kept saving them for later. And he told me, when I was all done, that I had a hell of a story to tell and that it was the kind of story he'd like to bring to the attention of the reading public.

"You be sure you put all the sex in," he said. "What you have to do is hook the reader's attention and rivet his eyes to the page right from the start, and then you make him laugh and cry by tugging at his heartstrings, but if you want to sell books, you'd better make sure you write something that'll give the son of a bitch a hard-on."

And he said he would take a chance on me.

"I'm a gambling man," he said. "I'm willing to take a risk. Now I'll tell you what I'll do. It won't take you long to write this all up, but you'll need something to live on in the meantime. You got a typewriter?" I didn't. "Well, you got to have a typewriter and money to live on. I figure you ought to be able to get a decent typewriter for twenty dollars. And living expenses—suppose I give you fifty bucks total, and you'll see how it goes."

I finally found a typewriter for thirty-five dollars. Not a very good typewriter, but since I can't type with more than two fingers, I suppose a good typewriter would be wasted on me. That left me with fifteen dollars, plus the dollar for changing the flat tire, plus the few dollars I had set aside.

Now Mr. Burger is supposed to read this, if he remembers who I am. And if he likes it he can publish it, and then I'll get some money, I guess. I don't know exactly how it works but I must get something. I've been killing myself writing all this, though I suppose it doesn't show when you read it. I don't suppose it's very good, either. And I probably put in either too much sex or not enough, and I don't even know which. And I'm sure I told you too many things you didn't want to know and skipped things you would have wanted to hear more about, but I never did this before.

And that's the whole point, actually, now that I

think about it. The first time is the hardest. There are probably other morals, too, but as sure as I like epilogues, I hate it when the author steps in at the end of the book and tells you what it was all about. Either you find it out for yourself or it's not worth knowing about. So I'll just say good-bye and thanks for reading this, and I'm sorry it wasn't better than it was.

Don't miss Lawrence Block's second
Chip Harrison novel,

CHIP HARRISON
SCORES AGAIN

Coming from Signet next spring.
Turn the page for a preview....

ONE

AT FIRST I DIDN'T PAY VERY MUCH ATTEN-
tion to the guy. I was washing my hands in the
men's room of a movie theater on Forty-second
Street, and in a place like that it's not an especially
good idea to pay too much attention to anybody
or you could wind up getting more involved than
you might want to. It's not that everybody is a
faggot. But everybody figures everybody *else* is a
faggot, so if you let your eyes roam around you
could get (*a*) groped by someone who's interested
or (*b*) punched in the mouth by someone who's
not interested or (*c*) arrested by someone who's
a cop.

If any of these things happened I would have
had to leave the theater, probably, and I didn't

want to. I had already seen both movies, one of them twice, but I still didn't want to leave. It was warm in the theater. Outside it was cold, with day-old snow turning from gray to black, and once I went out there I would have to stay out there, because I had no other place to go.

(Which is not entirely true. There was this apartment on East Fifth Street between Avenues B and C where I could stay if I really had to. Some friends of mine lived there, and while it wasn't exactly a crash pad they would always let me have a section of floor to sleep on and a plate of brown rice to eat. They were into this macrobiotic thing and all they ever ate was brown rice, which is very nourishing and very healthy and very boring after not very long. I could go there and eat and sleep and even talk to people, although most of the people you found there were usually too stoned to say very much, but the thing was that I only had a quarter, which is a nickel less than the subway costs. It was too cold to walk that far, and it was just about as cold inside that place as it was outside, because there was no heat. My friends had been using the stove to heat the place. That hadn't worked too well in the first place, and it worked less well when Con Ed turned off the gas and electricity for nonpayment. They burned candles for light and cooked the rice over little cans of Sterno. A couple of times Robbo had burned old furniture in the bathtub for heat, but he had more or less given this up, partly because heating the bathroom didn't do much for the rest of the apartment, and partly because there was a good chance the whole building would go up sooner or later.)

The point of this is just that I was washing my hands and not paying much attention to anything else until I happened to notice this guy take a wallet out of his pocket and start going through it. He was sort of hunched toward me, screening the wallet with his body from the washroom attendant, who I think existed to make sure that if anybody did anything dirty, they did it in one of the pay toilets. The guy with the wallet went through all the compartments of the thing, taking out money and plastic cards and things, and jamming everything into his pockets. Then he put the wallet in another pocket, took out a comb, combed his long dark hair back into a d.a., and left.

I turned and watched him, and on the way out his hand dipped into a pocket and came up with the wallet and dropped it into the wastebasket. There was this huge wastebasket on the opposite side of the door from the washroom attendant, and the guy with the d.a. did this whole number in one graceful motion, and the attendant never saw what happened.

I have to admit that it took me a minute to figure this out. Why would a guy throw his wallet away? And why be so slick about it? I mean, if you grow tired of your wallet, you have a perfect right to throw it away, right?

Oh.

It wasn't his wallet. He was a pickpocket or a mugger or something, and he had emptied the wallet, and now he wanted to get rid of it because it was Incriminating Evidence.

How about that.

My first reaction was just general excitement. Not that I had been an eyewitness to the most spectacular crime since the Brink's robbery. I would guess they get more wallets in those wastebaskets than they get paper towels. In fact, if you ever want a used wallet, that's probably the best place to go looking for one. But my own life hadn't been that thrilling lately, and it didn't take much to make my day.

The next thing that struck me was that I, Chip Harrison, had just been presented with an opportunity. A small one, perhaps, but I was as low on opportunities as I was on excitement. And that wallet was an opportunity.

It might hold important papers, for example. You might argue that people with important papers in their wallets don't spend all that much time in Forty-second Street movie houses, but one never knows for sure. Perhaps the owner would pay a reward for the return of the wallet. (Perhaps he'd call the police and have me arrested as a pickpocket.) Or perhaps there was some small change in the change compartment, if there was a change compartment. Or a subway token. Or a postage stamp. The Post Office won't redeem unused stamps, but at least I could mail a letter, if there was someone I wanted to write to. Or perhaps—

Well, there were endless possibilities.

I mulled them over in my mind while I was drying my hands on a paper towel, and I looked at the attendant and at the wastebasket, and then I went and combed my hair again. I had just done this before washing my hands in the first place and while my hair tends to need combing frequently it didn't really need it now. But I was about to Take Advantage of Opportunity, and thus I had to Think On My Feet.

I dried my hands again, and I carried the used paper towel over to the wastebasket, keeping the comb in the same hand with it, and I dropped them both into the basket.

Then I took a step or two toward the door, stopped abruptly, made a fist in one hand and hit the palm of the other hand with it.

"Oh, shit," I said. "I dropped my comb in the wastebasket."

"I seen you," the attendant said.

"All the stupid things."

"You want another comb, there's a machine over on the side."

"I want *that* comb," I said.

"Prob'ly dirty by now. You wouldn't believe the crap they throw in those baskets."

"I think I can get it." I was leaning into the basket and pawing around through old Kleenex and paper towels. The wallet had plummeted through them to the bottom, and I was having a hell of a time finding it.

"Over there," the clown said helpfully. "You see it?"

I did, damn him. I pawed at some paper towels and made the comb slip away. "Almost had it," I said, and went diving for it again. I had my feet off the ground and was balanced rather precariously, with the edge of the can pushing my belt buckle through my stomach. I had visions of losing my balance and winding up headfirst in the trashcan, which might provide some people with some laughs but which wouldn't provide me with the wallet, the comb, or much in the way of self-respect.

And self-respect, at that point of time, was as hard to come by as excitement, opportunity, and money.

I kept my balance and after another few shots I got the wallet. I can't swear that it's the same wallet I saw go in. For all I know there were a dozen of them somewhere down there. I got *a* wallet, palmed it off, and slipped it inside my shirt, and then I had to go through the charade of getting the fucking comb. It just didn't seem right to leave it there.

On my way through the lobby I dumped the comb in yet another wastebasket. And did it very surreptitiously, as if I were, well, a pickpocket ditching a wallet. Which is nothing but stupid.

I went outside and walked down to Broadway and watched the news flashing on the Allied Chemical Tower. It was cold, and there was a miserable wind blowing off the Hudson. I stood there shivering. I was out in the cold with no way of getting back into the warm, and I had traded a perfectly adequate pocket comb for a wallet that someone else had already gone through once, and I wasn't entirely certain I had come out ahead on the deal.

*   *   *

The papers in that wallet weren't important enough to wrap fish in. There were a couple of cash register receipts from unidentified stores and a Chinese laundry ticket. There was a head-and-shoulders snapshot of an ugly high school girl signed *Your Pal, Mary Beth Hawkins*. Judging by the hair style, Mary Beth was either (*a*) the squarest teen-ager in America or (*b*) forty-five years old by now. Either way, I would have rather had my comb than her picture.

There were a few other things, but none of them mattered except for the bus ticket. It was in one of the secret compartments, and I guess that had kept it a secret from the pickpocket. A Greyhound bus ticket, good for one-way passage in either direction between Boston, Massachusetts, and Bordentown, South Carolina. It said it was valid anytime within one year from the date stamped on the back. The date was March something, and it was now December something, so the ticket had another three months to go before it became even more worthless than it already was.

I got rid of the rest of the wallet, Mary Beth's picture and all. I dumped it in a trashcan—what else?—and I was as slick as possible about this, because I didn't want any other poor clown to waste his time doing what I had just done. If you're going to steal a wallet, you ought to get it from its original owner. After that the depreciation is fantastic.

Then I walked around for a while, which kept me warmer than standing still, if just barely. Now and then I would take the ticket out and stare at it. It was that or stare at the quarter. Sensational, I thought. If I happen to be in Boston between now and March, I can catch a bus to Bordentown. Or, should I some fine morning find myself in Bordentown, I can hop on a Greyhound for Boston. Wonderful.

I wound up on Broadway looking at whores. Not in a particularly acquisitive way. Not that I wasn't tempted. I had been in New York for almost three months, and my sex life during that time could have been inscribed on the head of a pin with plenty of room left for the Lord's Prayer and as many angels as felt like dancing there.

(I had been living with a girl for one of those three months, but she had just had a baby and couldn't do anything for six weeks, and by the time the six weeks were up she had gone away. At least she took the baby with her.)

I have always had these ethical objections to patronizing a prostitute, but in this case I might have overcome these objections if I'd had more than twenty-five cents to overcome them with. We'll never know.

So I went window-shopping, and the girls seemed to know it. They would look me up and down, and disapproval would glint in their eyes, and they would turn away, as if there was nothing so obvious as the fact that I couldn't possibly afford them. None of this was very ego-building.

And then one girl, who was either less experienced or a poorer judge of character, gave me a smile. An actual smile. So I stopped dead and smiled back at her, and she asked me if I'd like to go to her apartment.

"Is it warm there?"

"Honey," she said, "where I am, it's always warm."

I told her it sounded great. She asked me if I could spend twenty-five dollars.

"No way."

"Well, see, I like you. Could you spend twenty?"

"I wish I could."

"Well, shit. What *can* you spend?"

I could spend twenty-five cents, but I was damned if I was going to tell her that. I said, "Where are you from?"

"What do you want to know that for?"

"I just wondered."

"Well, I have this place on Fifty-fifth Street. How much can—"

"I mean originally," I said. "You're not from New York, are you?"

"From Memphis," she said. "And never goin' back there again, thanks all the same."

"Oh," I said.

"Why?"

"I thought maybe you were from Bordentown, South Carolina," I said. "Or maybe from Boston."

"You been drinkin', honey?"

"Because I have this bus ticket," I said, and showed it to her. "So if you had any interest in going to Boston or Bordentown—"

"That good?"

I showed her the date. "Perfectly good," I said.

"You want to come home with me?"

"To Memphis?"

"Shit. I tol' you. Fifty-fifth Street. You want to come?"

I tried on a smile. "All I really have is this ticket," I said. "I don't have any money. Just twenty-five cents and this ticket. I'm sorry for wasting your time—"

But she had my arm tucked under hers. "You

know something? I like you. I really do. What's your name?"

"Chip."

"Yeah? I'm Mary Beth. What's the matter?"

"Nothing. I knew a girl named Mary Beth. I had a picture of her in a wallet that I carried for a while."

"Girl here in New York?"

"No," I said. "I think she lives in Bordentown. Or in Boston. Or she used to."

"You sure you all right?"

"I'm fine," I said. She was still holding onto my arm, and we seemed to be walking uptown, sort of toward Fifty-fifth Street, actually.

"I do like you, Chip," she was saying. "You just come home with me and I'll do you like you never been done. You ever had something called the Waterloo? That's a specialty of mine. What I take is a mouthful of warm water, see—"

She told me quite a bit about the Waterloo, and while she talked we walked, and while we walked she held onto my arm and rubbed it against her breast. My pants began getting very cramped.

"You just forget about no money," she said. "Don't make no never mind."

Oh, Jesus, I thought. I can't believe this.

Because I couldn't. I mean, it wasn't as though I

hadn't had thoughts along this line before. I don't suppose it's the rarest fantasy ever. The ultimate sexual ego trip—that a prostitute, a girl who spends her life getting paid to have sex, will find you so overwhelmingly attractive that she'll want to give it to you for free. And she would know tricks you never dreamed of, and do all these fantastic things, and do them all for love.

Who ever thought it would actually happen?

Her apartment was pleasant in a sort of dull way. I couldn't tell whether or not it was a typical prostitute's apartment, but it seemed to me then that it couldn't be, because it seemed to me then that she was by no means a typical prostitute. By the time we got there I had already decided that she wasn't basically a whore at all. Just because a girl was whoring didn't make her a whore. After all, in the past year I had sold termite extermination service, picked fruit, posed for pornographic pictures and written a book, and I didn't think of myself as a writer or fruitpicker or any of those things. Life deals unpredictable cards, and you have to play each hand as it lays, and little Mary Beth might be walking the streets but that didn't make her a street-walker. It might not make her the Virgin Mary, either, but it didn't make her a whore.

I really had things all figured out. I would Take Her Away From All This. She already loved me, and by the time I got done balling her she would love me to distraction, and at that point the idea of ever having sex with anyone but Chip Harrison would positively turn her stomach. And I would live with her and land a Job With A Future, and we would screw incessantly while I made my way in the world, and we would, uh, Live Happily Ever After.

The thing is, see, that when a fantasy starts coming true before your eyes, it's natural to go on taking the fantasy to its logical (?) conclusion. Did I really expect all of this would happen? Not really, but remember that I never expected it to start happening in the first place. If someone goes and repeals the Law of Gravity and you find yourself flying to the Moon, it's no more unreasonable to plan on flying clear through to Mars.

I stood there working all of this out while she closed the door and turned four or five locks. Doesn't want us to be interrupted, I thought happily. We might be there for days. Weeks. And she wants to make sure we have privacy.

"Well," she said. "Not much, but it's home."

"Mary Beth," I said.

"Hi, Chip."

"Mary Beth." And I put my hands on her shoulders and drew her close. Somewhere along the way her head turned to the side and I was kissing a gold hoop ear-ring.

"Uh-uh," she said.

She rubbed her breasts against my chest and bounced her groin playfully against mine. I had this tight feeling in my chest.

"I don't kiss on the mouth," she said.

"Huh?"

She gave me another happy bounce, then moved away. "Just something I don't do," she said. "Kiss you anywhere else, kiss you like nobody ever, but not on the mouth."

"But that's silly."

"Shit—"

"But—"

I remembered reading that some prostitutes refused to kiss their clients mouth-to-mouth. They would do anything else, but they reserved that intimacy for the men they loved. It had never made much sense to me at the time, because if you stop and think about it, well, it's pretty ridiculous. Especially since I had spent the past year with a lot of girls who would kiss you mouth-to-mouth until Rome fell but wouldn't do anything more exciting than that. It seemed as though the whores had their value system turned upside down.

But what I couldn't understand was what this had to do with me and Mary Beth. She didn't want money from me. She was doing this for love, so by rights she should be particularly keen on kissing me on the mouth.

And then I got it. The poor kid, I realized, had never really had any sex life to speak of outside of prostitution. So naturally that was her frame of reference. Here she wanted to ball me for the sheer unadulterated pleasure of it, but her mind was so conditioned by the life she led that she had to act with me in much the same way as she acted with her paying customers. It was weird, and sort of disheartening in a way, but there was also something sort of sweet and pathetic about it.

She has never known love, I told myself. But I shall change her. I shall fulfill her.

"Well, now," she said. "And what have we here?"

That must have been a rhetorical question, because what we had there was something she came into contact with quite frequently in her profession, and where we had it was in her hand. She had opened my fly and taken me firmly in hand, and she was stroking me rhythmically. Her wrist did everything; the rest of her arm stayed motionless.

"You come with me," she said. "We'll just wash you up first."

We stood at the bathroom sink and washed me up. The editorial *we* was bugging me a little. Nurses talk like that—"How are we feeling this morning?"—but I never figured whores did, too. Anyway, she soaped me up and rinsed me off, and it was sort of pleasant and unpleasant both at once, pleasant in that it felt good, and unpleasant in that it sort of implied that I was fundamentally too dirty to deal with otherwise. But then I thought of some of the things she had in mind, and some of the things she had done with other people, and I decided I was just as glad that she tended to wash this portion of a person beforehand, and also, to tell the truth, just as pleased that she didn't believe in mouth-to-mouth kissing.

When she was done she filled a glass with hot water and carried it into the bedroom. "For the Waterloo," she explained. "You're gonna love this."

"Uh."

"Don't you want to take off your clothes, Chip?"

"Uh, sure," I said, and started undressing. I was

feeling unbelievably dizzy and stupid, and it wasn't just the excitement. That was a part of it. But another part was the feeling that none of this was really happening. It all seemed so thoroughly unreal. I took off all my clothes and looked up and she was just standing there, with her clothes on.

"Your clothes," I said.

"Huh?"

"Why don't you, uh, get undressed?"

"You want me to?"

"Well, sure."

She shrugged. A very strange girl, I decided. Maybe it wasn't just that she hadn't had any real sex life outside of prostitution. Maybe she was equally inexperienced *in* prostitution. Maybe she just read about the Waterloo in a book or something.

I stood there watching while she got undressed. She didn't make the process particularly seductive, just shucked off her clothes and draped them over a chair. Her body was skimpy everywhere but the breasts, which were on the large size. I haven't described her too much because I have trouble picturing her now in my mind. She was sort of mousy, really, hair somewhere between blond and brown. I suppose she was around my age, although she seemed older, maybe because she was more at home in this scene than I was.

She left on her stockings and garter belt. I asked her if she didn't want to take them off and get comfortable, and she gave me an impatient look. "Most men like 'em on," she said. "Don't you think they look pretty?"

I thought they looked like something out of those whip-and-chain movies, but I said sure, they were pretty.

"Because it's wasting time, you know, taking 'em off, putting 'em on."

"Then leave them on," I said, and she nodded, and I reached out for her and drew her in close. I went to kiss her again, out of habit, but she turned away automatically and I didn't press the point. I sort of felt like apologizing but couldn't think of an intelligent way to do that, so I kept my mouth shut and let my fingers do the walking. I felt various parts of her, and she did a little deep breathing and such, but nothing that really assured me I was driving her out of her skull.

"Let me," she said, disengaging herself. "You just lay down, Chip, and let me do you up."

I got on the bed. She reached for the glass of water, then stopped with it halfway to her lips. "You tell me if it's too hot," she said.

Then she took a mouthful of water and bent over me.

It was really very nice. She just did it for a second or so, then pulled away and looked at me. I was waiting for her to ask me whatever the hell it was she was going to ask me, and then I realized that she wasn't going to ask me anything because she couldn't because she had her mouth full of hot water.

"It's not too hot," I said. "It's just right."

She nodded and started doing it again. And, as before, it was really very nice indeed. It was strange, too, because I felt totally unconnected with the whole process. I decided that it was a great technique, and it was really great that she knew these great techniques, but that it would be infinitely better when I taught her how to put some love into the whole process. Or at least to make it obvious to me that she was enjoying what she was doing.

Then she stopped again.

"Believe me, it's not too hot," I said, and started to push her head back in place. But her head wouldn't push. She leaned over and spat the water out onto the linoleum.

"The ticket," she said.

"Huh?"

She looked impatient again. "The bus ticket, man. You better give it to me now. I want to make sure it's still good."

"The bus ticket?"

She sat up and stared at me. "Shit, the *bus* ticket," she said. "What's the matter with you? You got to give it to me and I got to make sure I can cash it before we do any more. All I need is—"

"Cash the bus ticket?"

"Take it over to Port Authority and cash it," she said. "I told you you didn't need money. Just the ticket is all. If it's good I'll get twenty-thirty dollars out of that ticket."

I suppose you saw it coming all along, but I'm not going to apologize for my stupidity. After all, it was *my* fantasy that we were acting out.

The Waterloo, I thought. I had already had the hot water part, and now I was getting the cold water. Buckets of it, all over all my enthusiasm for little old Mary Beth.

"Hey! Where you goin'?"

I was putting on my clothes. Not too quickly, not too slowly. Very mechanically, actually. Tucking the shirt into the pants, getting my socks rightside out and then putting them on, then the shoes—

"You crazy?"

"I have to go," I said.

"Go? Where to?"

'The bus station," I said. "I have to cash the ticket."

"Shit, I said I would cash it. Just hand it on over here."

"Fuck you," I said.

"Are you out of your *mind?*"

I turned toward her, and I guess I must have wanted to kill her, or at least I looked as though I wanted to kill her, because her face drained of color and she backed off fast. I turned away from her again and went to the door.

The whore with the heart of gold. You didn't need money. All you needed was a negotiable bus ticket.

I almost went crazy unlocking all those locks. She never said a word, which was lucky for her. I'm normally about as non-violent as it's possible to get, but I wasn't feeling very normal just then. Nothing makes you hate a person quite so much as being made an absolute asshole out of.

The last lock cleared just as I was about to give up and kick the door down.

It was as cold as ever out there, but I walked three blocks before I even noticed it.

Two thoughts kept me from running around and screaming. One was that, if and when I calmed down, I was certain to see the humor in the situation. I didn't see any humor in it now, but I knew I would sooner or later.

The other comforting thought, and it was the more comforting of the two, was that I had that bus ticket in my pocket. And I could cash it in.